Old Love

Copyright © 2021 by Nancy J. Hedin

Bella Books, Inc.
P.O. Box 10543
Tallahassee, FL 32302

Printed in the United States of America on acid-free paper.

First Bella Books Edition 2021

Editor: Medora MacDougall
Cover Designer: Heather Honeywell

ISBN: 978-1-64247-231-8

Old Love

The Best Barbeque Sauce in the World

Nancy J. Hedin

BELLA
B O O K S
2021

Acknowledgments

My sincere thanks to the women and men of Swanville, Minnesota, for their tireless work planning and implementing the Swanville Midsummer Carnival. The work of these service clubs, volunteers, and faithful carnival attendees has kept Swanville thriving. Special thanks to the Lions Club, the Women's Club, Legion Auxiliary, and Dollars for Scholars for their generosity, focus on education, and vision.

There are details in this novel graciously provided by Con Natvig and Bruce Johnson. Both men promptly answered my questions and everything that is accurately described is to their credit. Mistakes or misrepresentations are mine alone.

I chose to use some of the surnames I remember from Swanville. I used them with affection and respect. Any character that appeared in bad light or dubious intentions, I made up from whole cloth. My neighbors are kind and good.

Thank you, Bella Books, for bringing *Old Love* into the world. Thank you, Linda Hill and Jessica Hill. Thank you, Medora MacDougall, for your edits and collaboration. You helped make the book better and you made doing that fun.

Dedication

All my writing is dedicated to my wife, Tracy, and our daughters, Sophia and Emma, and in honor of my parents, Edwin and RoJean Hedin; my siblings, Kathy, Lin, Michael, and David, and my grandmothers, Amanda Tall and Mary Hedin. I could not create what I have made without your love, support, and influence.

I would also like to dedicate this novel to my aunt Wilma, who is the best cook in the county and has nourished generations of people in Swanville. Wilma is generous, kind, and humble. She exemplifies what I remember about living in a small town.

Likewise, I dedicate this novel to my uncle Russ, who influenced me greatly. He personifies grace, gregariousness, and good manners. He and his mother, Amanda Tall, encouraged me to seek as much education as I could.

As you might expect, having great aunts and uncles leads to wonderful cousins. I love all of mine and hope they each see themselves here in this dedication. I especially pay tribute to Janet, Sandy, Kathy, and Cindy, who were my friends during my childhood and my supporters during adulthood. This book is for you too. I didn't see my city cousins and Washington cousins much over the years, but I wish to include them in this dedication because the few times we got together, they were nothing less than kindness and love on a stick. And they read my books. Special call out to Barbara, Beth, Sarah, and Steven.

Additionally, this novel is dedicated to the town and people of Swanville, Minnesota. Swanville is my hometown and having grown up there informs all my writing. Swanville is a town where teachers come and stay for their whole career and even those people who move away come back to have a pop or beer and some barbequed chicken at the Midsummer Carnival.

CHAPTER ONE

Mary Caine and the General Store

The temperature outside was murderously hot. Mary Caine placed a bag of frozen peas on the back of her neck. She had considered using the frozen tater tots but that seemed just silly. As she watched out her store window, she complained to Mr. Bob Barker VI, "It's only late June and it's Africa hot and Southeast Asia humid."

She liked maps and global comparisons even if she'd never been outside of Minnesota and rarely away from her hometown of Whistler other than the four years she went to college in a city only two hours away. "The air is so thick this morning I have to chew it before I take it into my lungs. Do you know what I mean?"

Bob Barker VI didn't answer. The smelly, brown and white Springer Spaniel groaned and repositioned himself on the cool linoleum floor. Every dog Mary owned had been named for the star of *The Price Is Right* because Bob Barker was her father's favorite game show host. The name was first homage, then a joke, and then a sad convenience when her father started losing his memory.

"And another thing, 'Hot enough for you?' I'd about liked to strangle the next imbecile who says that to me. I'd do it too if I wouldn't be arrested and didn't have this store to run."

Binoculars hanging from her neck, Mary peered out the large sheet-glass windows of the grocery store her family had owned for three generations and she'd run alone since her dad died five years before.

"Dad would have made eighty-two last month if he hadn't died. Death keeps you young."

Mary prided herself on her death math. She could tell you how old her lost loved ones would have been if they hadn't been lost to her. "Mom, if she's alive somewhere, would be seventy-two this month."

She habitually threatened to close or sell the store and move away from Whistler. These were empty threats. Mary and all her neighbors knew she could never leave. It was a voluntary choice, although sometimes she behaved as if she were not a person but an inanimate object like a fence post pounded into the ground by an unseen force. She was a post in the ground without will or volition.

Still, some days, she wished to be anywhere else. She was tired of waiting and she wanted quiet. While in search of the sounds of silence Mary had retained her personal computer, but she'd hoisted her TV out the upstairs window into the store's Dumpster below. She paid the trash hauler a couple sirloin steaks that were about to go off to dispose of the shattered TV properly, but Mary felt a great sense of relief. She didn't want to hear any voices blathering on unless they needed to buy something from her general store or if they had something to say about the Midsummer Carnival. Then, she'd listen. Then it was important.

The truth was Mary Caine was restless because she had heard Sadie Barnes had moved back to Whistler. "Sadie. Say it loud and there's music playing; say it soft and it's almost like praying." Mary stole the old Leonard Bernstein lyrics to announce her own westside story. She and Sadie had been lovers a lifetime ago when Sadie and Mary were fresh out of college. Sadie had moved to Whistler to teach English.

Now Sadie had returned to take a job as the new high school superintendent. That gossip both excited and scared the hell out of Mary. There was plenty of hell left in Mary, but she had felt a quart low since the news and didn't know if her heart could take seeing Sadie again.

That wasn't exactly it. Her heart would sing to see Sadie again, but it would stop, frozen in her chest, if Sadie left again.

The store was empty. The morning rush—ten to twelve customers needing something before their morning work commute to bigger towns with industry—had petered out. Mary had counted the money in the till and reviewed her bank statement three times. Like her father she penny pinched, stretched the dollar and every other metaphor for stinginess disguised as frugality. Her closed-fisted attitude with money was not a character defect she hadn't yet detected in herself. She'd found it, others had pointed it out, and she'd noted the family resemblance for quite a while. She shared the trait with her father as surely as she had his brown eyes and straight teeth. Skimping was still a hard habit to break or "rabbit to bake" as her father had said when he was three sheets to the wind drunk.

Her breakfast of oatmeal and cinnamon toast was eaten. She felt hungry again but restrained herself from eating into profits. She'd read from her morning affirmation book and prayed to her Higher Power to not drink and be of service to her fellows. Mary wrote a quote for the day on the store blackboard, "In a world where you can be anything, be kind"—author unknown.

It was almost ten o'clock. Mary was counting the days until the Midsummer Carnival. "A week from this Friday, my friends. Then we'll have Lions Club barbequed chicken, Women's Civic Club pies, and Legion Auxiliary hamburgers. It's a feast I tell you, and that's besides all the food trucks that accompany the Midway outfit. It's a new company this year named something like, Transformation Amusements. That's curious, don't you think?"

Mary eyed the yellow cat that rested in the store's front window next to the sale display of bug dope, sunscreen, and cup coolers. "Vanna White, just thinking makes me sweat! How can you stand wearing that fur coat?" Vanna White licked her undercarriage and completely ignored Mary, as was Vanna White's style and the habit of every cat Mary and her father employed. "I'd take off all my clothes if I wouldn't be subjected to ridicule and possibly an arrest."

Nothing. Vanna White lifted a back leg out. The gesture gave Mary cramping up her own leg into her butt. The cat licked her upper thighs. Mary couldn't watch any more. Vanna White's only job, beyond the extermination of mice, was to look pretty and she did so without the benefit of sequins, heels, or the faintest concept of word puzzles.

"I believe I'll eat a bag of mini donuts every day and two bags on any day I don't eat cheese curds." She put both hands on her belly.

"Gospel truth," Win squawked from his perch in an oversized cage that hung from a chain bolted to the ceiling in the front of the store. As opposed to Vanna White, Mary's pet crow shined to word games.

Mary smiled with pride as she rewarded the winged mimic with a peanut in a shell. "See if you remember this one?" She began reading crossword puzzle clues to Edwin, "Win" for short, a crow she'd raised since he first fell from a nest in one of the red pine trees that skirted the parking lot of Mary's store.

Today, truth be told, Mary was perturbed at Win. He'd stayed out all night the night before. She had told him time and time again, "Be back by store closing time or I'm locking the door." She had patrolled the skies with her binoculars for him for a full two hours past closing, and he hadn't returned. The next morning, she found him loitering on the front steps of the store like nothing had happened. He was disheveled. Detritus he'd likely found or stolen hung from his beak like icicles. Win was a carousing thief, but she played with him anyway.

"Four down, six letters, life cut short by foul play."

Win pursed his beak, looked off in the distance through the bars of his open cage like he was worrying at the problem. If he planned to answer, he didn't. The store door swung open wildly, the bells above the door clanging that there was a customer. Mary was so glad for the breeze that she didn't scold the patron for letting the air conditioning out.

"They found two bodies." Perspiration was beaded on the boy's acne-peppered face. "Dead. Do you think that will mess up the Carnival?"

Bob Barker's eyes perked up. The hound yawned. Win squawked, "Murder."

"What bodies? And why would that mess up the Carnival?" Mary gave another peanut to Win and then concentrated her attention on the boy.

The boy's head swiveled to look at the shiny, black bird, but he continued his tale. "There's two dead bodies down by the dock. My phone died." He waved a small, flat, black thing at Mary. "Can I use your phone to call home?"

The boy was short of breath. Mary supposed it was to be expected. He'd probably run to the store from the lake and he spoke of two deaths in one sentence. He approached Mary's counter and pointed at one of the last landlines in the world, a harvest gold wall phone with an extra-long cord so that Mary could take inventory, order stock from any aisle of the store, and of course look out the window in case someone interesting walked by.

"Go ahead." Mary nodded toward the phone. She despised cell phones even before the stories about risks for brain cancer. She refused to squander her money on one and she detested the notion that if she had one, she would be expected to answer it and always be available. It seemed like elevating her importance to that of a deity and Mary knew she was no god.

Bob Barker barked.

She talked with her crow but understood her dog as well. She turned to Bob Barker and scowled. "Slow your roll, pup. We aren't going fishing at the dock." To the store, the universe, and God Mary said, "Nobody better mess up the Carnival."

The dog put his head down and covered his eyes with his paws. Mary turned to the crow. "You got four down. How about a 1960 Alfred Hitchcock film with a famous shower scene?"

The high school boy was dressed in last year's Carnival T-shirt. He must have worked on setup the year prior. The Whistler Lions Club bought the shirts to give to volunteers. Mary had one in every color and in every design since the

Carnival's inception when she was a child; her favorite one was yellow with a white vinyl drawing of a Ferris wheel over her left breast.

Just the thought of the Carnival made Mary's heart race and teeth itch in excitement and anticipation. She could almost smell the chicken, slathered with the best barbeque sauce in the world, grilling in the chicken shack. The food at the Carnival was Mary's only financial extravagance. She never touched her inheritance from her grandma. That was to sustain her in her old age, and her savings—all her recent profit from the store—was intended for a roof garden that would provide organic produce to the store at a reduced cost.

Suddenly, she was thirsty for beer. Not just any beer, but beer tapped from a keg that had been chilled by ice cut from Lake Pepin last January. Her breath came fast, and she had to wipe the corners of her mouth just thinking about the amber refreshment. She convulsed like Bob Barker expelling water from his coat. She put that thought of beer out of her mind. She was forever a drunk, but she didn't drink anymore. She sighed, lost in her memories, and warded off the self-pity of revisiting her drunken regrets.

"Ma, this is Jimmy."

Mary startled, remembering that the boy was in the store and had a connection to the outside world and a tale to tell. She recognized him. Well, not really. She was familiar with his production company. He was a Royce. She couldn't have identified which one. The Royces were like Chevys—a new model every year. The models didn't differ much from year to year and she assumed they were all pretty much the same under the hood—fairly reliable. Were they one of the families that felt compelled to use the same first letter for every child's name? She didn't know. She hoped not.

Mary listened in on the boy's conversation. It wasn't like it was eavesdropping—it was her store, her phone.

"Yes, Mom. I signed up for every work crew they had, but please don't come get me just yet." He looked over at Mary and crossed his fingers. "County sheriff's in town. They found two dead bodies down at the dock—one in the water and the other up on shore."

If Jimmy used his definite articles correctly Mary reasoned that the bodies had been found at the community dock and boat landing. It wasn't "Hutchin's dock" or "Howard's dock" on Little Swan but "the dock." That likely meant that the body was found by the public landing on Lake Pepin, a few blocks from the store. *Interesting*.

From the sighs, eye rolling, and whiny tone that came next, she got the impression that Jimmy's mom had said her boy could not remain in town longer even at the promise of glimpsing dead bodies.

Win shook his feathered head side to side in derision. "Psycho."

Jimmy again looked suspiciously at the winged, black squawk box.

"Some people would argue it is one of his best films," Mary said to Win, more from wanting to show off his trick than any conviction about the movie.

"Bullshit!" The bird's voice was a rusty hinge.

"Does that bird really know the answers to that puzzle?" the boy asked.

"He's showing off for you. We both were. We solved this puzzle together last week." Mary pointed at the boy. "You want to see the dead bodies, don't you?"

The boy nodded.

"I get it. You haven't seen many dead bodies and few without fur, feathers, or scales. Those of us older"— she didn't tell him that she was creeping up on the front side of sixty— "we've already seen too much death."

A quarter of Mary's high school classmates had passed. Her birth mother was as good as dead. Mary'd barely ever met her and had no conscious memories of her that weren't seeded and likely embellished by her father. Some stories were verified by photographs in an old album upstairs.

"My father passed five years ago. A stroke. He would have been eighty-two last month." Mary didn't know how those who had served their country in the military, police, or fire ever slept with the parade of dead bodies they had in their heads. The absent ones in her own life haunted her daily.

"I don't care to see another dead body, unless it's my own and I can hover above and see who gets stuck making the goulash and box cake mixes for my funeral. Actually, that's not true. I don't want the excessive expense of a funeral lunch. If there's anyone who wants to send me off, they can eat at home before they come. I want to be cremated and dumped out the window of a fast-moving car driving around Little Swan Lake."

"Okay." Jimmy's forehead knitted up. "Thanks," he said, head down, shoulders slumped as he lumbered toward the door.

"Jimmy, what do these dead bodies have to do with canceling the Carnival?"

"I don't exactly know, but the sheriff said maybe it was a serial killer."

"Are you kidding me? A serial killer in Whistler, Minnesota? Sheriff Spelt is an ignoramus, no offense to other ignoramuses or his parents who had anticipated a far superior dunce."

"I don't know. The sheriff was really angry because he said killers should have the common decency to kill just one person at a time."

"Right. The first thing you think about when it comes to murder is common decency." Mary chuckled slightly at the sheriff's sloth, but she felt heartsick thinking of any of her neighbors being dead and felt worse to think that any of them were murdered. "Did you see anything?"

"No! I mean, sorta."

"Sorta?"

"One dead guy was on the lakeshore. I didn't get to see anything but his feet. He had big feet."

"You know what they say about big feet?"

"What?"

"Never mind."

"He wore black dress shoes. The sheriff had him covered with a tarp. The other body was in the water—bobbing there like a floatie at swimming lessons. The sheriff poked at it with a long pole. I suppose he was trying to get it to float closer to the dock. Then the sheriff yelled at the girl deputy to wade out and haul the body out of the water. It didn't look like a person in the water, but it did once it was pulled to shore." The boy's eyes widened. "It was someone local. That's what people are saying."

"What color clothes?"

"Blue. Jeans and a shirt."

"Man or woman?"

"Man." The boy looked more closely at Mary, who wore blue jeans and an oversized, blue men's work shirt. "Or a woman. I guess, but I can't say for certain."

"There must have been some talk about who it was?" Mary knew folks in Whistler could identify their own at fifty paces by clothes alone unless the corpse was wearing a Whistler Wildcat jersey. Then it could be just about anybody and a closer vantage point would be required for proper identification.

"I heard somebody say it looked like the 'Latiskee mistake,' Ms. Caine." Jimmy cocked his head like a golden retriever. "What's a Latiskee mistake?"

Mary could think of several correct answers to Jimmy's question. She wracked her brain for something positive or at least neutral to say, like she was devising answers for a multiple-choice test.

She could say that Latiskee was the name of a family who lived north of town. The small spread's roadside appeal flashed immediately into Mary's brain. Their farm was neat and tidy. The machinery—mostly John Deere—was parked in a straight line between the barn and a row of Norway spruce trees. Another row of closely planted balsam fir trees created a natural windbreak on the other side of the property. The fields were plowed, planted, and harvested promptly. Their gardens' black soil enriched with chicken manure nourished vegetables, berry bushes, and fruit trees.

Mary had heard that Old Man Latiskee, the patriarch of the family, shot at people who drove or stepped on his property uninvited. Even the school bus driver had parked a hundred yards from the end of Latiskee's long, paved driveway for fear that Latiskee would shoot him during the morning pickup or afternoon drop-off. The story was legend, but not necessarily true.

The reference to a *mistake* probably meant it was the last boy, Lloyd, known to most as Buddy, who graduated a few years ago. It was a cruel way of making mention of an unplanned pregnancy. Mary suspected there were plenty of mistakes living their lives just fine. She often felt she must be one. Otherwise, why would her mother have left?

The other Latiskee children were grown and gone to out-of-state colleges when Lloyd was born. He lived in town. Mary had seen him, of course, but she couldn't tell Jimmy a useful thing about him other than possibly a fairly accurate reconstructed memory of his grocery list.

Like her neighbors, Mary had never been invited to the Latiskee place. She'd driven by eight or ten years ago when there was a rumor Martin Latiskee had invested in a few solar panels, and she had meandered that direction a year ago when she heard he installed a wind turbine. His forward thinking on energy added to Martin Latiskee's aura of mystery and danger. She wanted to drive up to the house and ask him if the technology was really worth the investment and how much was he saving, but she valued the way her head sat on her shoulders too much to set foot out there uninvited.

Sure, they'd shopped at her grocery store some, the General Store being the only grocery store in Whistler, but they rarely stopped in and only to barter for things they didn't already grow, raise, or cobble together themselves. It was rumored Martin Latiskee was an inventor of some profit and renown.

Mary remembered having taken freshly butchered chickens from Mrs. Latiskee's knotted, arthritic hands. The chickens were antibiotic-free and grass-fed and probably in better health than Lois herself or Mary for that matter.

Lois Latiskee was older than her husband, Martin. Her mouth, a slit underlining her red, chapped nose, never gave a hint if the bargain she'd struck with Mary pleased her. She just gathered up the toiletries, fabric, or nails she'd traded for and stuffed them in a burlap sack, nodded, and clomped out the door in leather work boots too big for her feet and never intended for her gender.

Mary had wished she could offer the woman an afternoon of an undisturbed bubble bath and nap—not that the woman wasn't clean. She was neat and clean, her red hair brushed to a sheen. Of course Mary didn't say anything about a bubble bath to her.

Mary looked at Jimmy as he waited patiently for her definition of a Latiskee. She sighed, "Latiskee is the name of a family of people who are part of our town."

"Oh." Jimmy left.

She supposed her reply temporarily answered the boy's question, but Mary's mind was buzzing with unsettled inquiries. Was it really the youngest Latiskee in the water? Why? How? Who was the other dead person? Why the hell hadn't Sadie Barnes been in Mary's store yet?

Mary flashed a prayer into the ether for the hearts that would be broken by these losses. She removed the binoculars from around her neck and placed them behind the counter. The store air felt even more suffocating than before Jimmy's arrival and unexpected tale. Technically, the store was air-conditioned. The machine poked out from the wall like a louvered wart. It made a racket like it was doing something. A coolish breeze emanated from it if Mary stood really close, but she suspected that the majority of cool air just rose up and tickled the tin ceiling tiles. She imagined dollar signs floating above her.

She swayed back and forth on her feet. She sat down. Her leg bounced and she began biting her nails. Even though she didn't want to see a dead body, curiosity and the futility of ever feeling cool got the best of her. She grabbed her store keys. She returned the bag of less than frozen peas to the freezer, nestling them in among the other bags of peas, frozen corn, and bags of vegetable medley.

"Come on, Bob." Bob popped up off the floor and stood by Mary.

Win paced on his perch and then said, "Hey, hey, hey."

"What?" Mary stood with hands on her hips and stared at the crow. "You want to come along too? You didn't get enough fresh air when you were gone all night last night? Come on, then." She wasn't as perturbed with the bird as she pretended to be. She envied the winged pirate. She wondered what it felt like to fly.

The big, black bird flew out of his cage; the door to the cage was rarely closed. He landed on the metal rack with the serving-size bags of potato chips, corn chips, and beer nuts, overpriced and ready for impulsive shoppers and overeaters. He waited on the display as Mary approached the front door.

"How about you, Vanna White? You want to see a dead body?" No answer. Mary flipped the plastic sign to read "Closed," turned out the lights, opened the door for Win and Bob Barker, followed them out, and locked the door. She scolded herself for the lost dollars in sales. On the bright side, her early closing might spark some speculation. That was worth something. She smiled to herself.

Win soared away into the cloudless morning sky, his wings extended and his feathers splayed like black gloves. He probably knew exactly where he was going. His receptive language was impressive even if his expressive language wasn't much more than what Mary had bribed him to mimic. Mary watched him briefly rise in the air, clear the tops of the buildings across Main Street and disappear in the direction of Lake Pepin. As she walked along the sidewalk she looked down at her clothes—blue jeans and blue chambray work shirt, sleeves rolled to above her dry, achy elbows.

"Hell, Bob, if I played my cards right and stayed out of sight, maybe somebody'd start the rumor the body floating in the water was mine, but what on earth was I doing with someone in dress shoes at Lake Pepin? Nope, that ruse wouldn't hold."

CHAPTER TWO

Whistler, MN

Brownstone and brick two-story buildings, some built as early as the 1880s when the railroad made it to the Whistler side of Big Falls, flanked both sides of Whistler's Main Street. Like stained teeth, Mary's General Store was part of the lower plate along with the senior center, library, funeral home, and an implement shop. Lake Pepin was a little more than four blocks from where her store stood. She jaywalked. She didn't pass directly in front of the businesses on the west side of the street: the bank, the old newspaper office, Rahn's Hardware, the Café, and the Municipal Liquor Store. She caught Second Street by the barbershop.

A penny on the ground caught her eye. She stooped to pick it up, her hand shaking and tightness coming to her chest from the herculean effort bending over that far had become. She looked at the penny—a wheat head from 1945. She clenched it in her hand a moment before placing it in her pocket. She felt lucky.

She peeked over the cedar picket fence to admire the barber's rock garden. A squadron of fat bumblebees and honeybees hovered and lit on the black-eyed Susans and coreopsis. Next, they buried their compound eyes and sucky tongues in the blooms of a blue hydrangea. A fountain burbled. Wind chimes played by the breeze tinkled a little song.

She crossed over an obsolete set of train tracks that looked like thick electrical cords running to the grain bins by the feedstore. She noted the creosote-covered railroad ties impervious to rot and disuse. They made her think of her father. He swore by the economy of creosote. "I should coat myself in the stuff, Mary. I'd live forever." Mary wished he were still with her.

As she walked through two ditches, grasshoppers hopped about and she suspected sneaky garden snakes slithered in the knee-high grasses, thistles, and coneflowers. Bob sniffed everything and pissed about every fifteen feet. She passed a few houses, the Oslunds' two-story, the same cheery color of yellow as the coreopsis in the barber's rock garden, and the Schmidts' white siding stark against the green of their neatly landscaped yard.

Mary stood at the edge of the Highway 28 blacktop and took in the scene. The water of Lake Pepin shown blue and peaceful as glass. A lighter blue sky rose above the green seam of trees and topped the lake like an open clam shell.

Just seven months prior the lake had been a frozen, windswept, white disk. She thought back to a January day when men from town used ice-cutting chainsaws to extract ten tons of ice for use at the Carnival. She had heard stories that her paternal grandfather had cut the ice on Little Swan with handheld cross saws to provide the ice for the local dance pavilion. The dance hall and her grandfather were long gone.

The ice cut from Lake Pepin in January was at that moment covered in sawdust and boxed in a wooden shed built for just that purpose. The ice waited to be of service, just like two hundred volunteers who prepared for their roles in the town's biggest event, the Midsummer Carnival.

God, how she loved the Carnival. She thought she should rightly hate the event. It was during Carnival that her mom had left Mary and her dad. Her mother had left with the midway outfit, the community equivalent of having left your family to join the circus. She wondered what her mom did for a traveling entertainment business and why it had been more attractive than staying in Whistler and making a life with Mary and her father. She wondered if it was her mother's trailblazing exodus that had broken some sort of membrane in the universe, making it easier for others, like Sadie, to leave Mary later.

On her more spiteful days she imagined her mom traveling with a circus as a bearded lady or a sword swallower. The midway outfit that came to Whistler didn't have freak shows, just rides, games, and deep-fried foods. Her mom having left with the carnies didn't embarrass Mary as much as give her hope that it would be the Carnival that would bring her mom back home again. She believed in romantic symmetry.

At the lake, quite a crowd had already gathered in the parking lot and small picnic area that fronted the public boat landing and municipal dock. The assemblage was held back from the crime scene with flimsy yellow plastic tape. It reminded Mary of the stories of cats fearing vacuum cleaner hoses. Anyone could easily break through the barrier but didn't from fear or propriety. Or maybe people were at times dumb as cats. The road was lined with American-made pickup trucks and sedans like nobody had jobs or obligations.

Her father would have said that it was an opportune time for burglars because half the town was out gawking at some damn thing. He would have been gawking too were he still alive. He'd have conscripted Mary to watch the store. He'd have driven the few blocks to the lake in his ancient baby blue Chevy pickup with the rusty, rotting floorboards that let dust and exhaust filter into the cab of the truck. Ed would have worn his seat belt or "rope" as he called it. The irony being that he also had an open can of beer in his nondriving hand and a six-pack on the seat. He'd have brought the remaining cold beer with him to the event and overcharged spectators for the cans he sold singly. He'd have freely shared a wisecrack or two. She missed him and let a tear make it halfway down her cheek before she wiped it away and raised her head higher.

She walked closer, scanning the crowd. She fell into the standing group of gawkers. It wasn't like there were bleachers for this event. She saw familiar faces, friends and neighbors, but she was looking for one face in particular. Sadie. She glanced over her shoulder to the high school. Maybe these doings were sad entertainment compared to the heady work of school administration. Then again, maybe the third-floor English room window was the best place to watch the mysterious gathering at the lake. Mary pictured *her* gazing through binoculars, but Mary's progressive-lensed bifocals didn't help her verify her suspicions. Still, Mary hoped that Sadie Barnes looked out from the windows of the high school, noticed Mary, and that Mary's butt looked good.

CHAPTER THREE

The Living and the Dead

The county coroner's white van/flower delivery truck motored by slowly, skirting the assembly of spectators. Sheriff Donald Spelt waved the vehicle in place and then sauntered over to it. He hitched up his pants before he bent at the waist and rested his forearms on the open van window, his belly dusting the driver's side door as he talked with Dr. Hanson, the coroner/ retired doctor/amateur taxidermist. Mary wasn't close enough to hear what was said.

Deputy Hart, the only female deputy in the county, stood hands on her hips, lake water dripping from poop-colored polyester dress pants which were now covered in dull green lake scum. Mary supposed Hart got all the shit jobs. In this particular scenario, as Jimmy had reported, that meant that Deputy Hart had had to wade into the murky, tepid soup that was Lake Pepin, retrieve the body, and drag it out to lie by the other body. Now she stood watch over the corpses, both shrouded by blue plastic tarps like firewood or out-of-season sporting gear.

Indistinct conversation and a few snicks from cell phone cameras accounted for most of the activity by onlookers.

Beyond the one corpse's identity and demise Mary imagined that several obvious questions hung in the air: Why would this death endanger the Carnival and who would cover the man's shifts if he was scheduled at the chicken shack, bingo hall, or beer garden? Who the hell was the other man? Did he have shifts at the Carnival as well? She thought it would be ironic if the wet corpse had a shift in the dunking booth, but she kept that thought to herself.

Win, that snoopy, kleptomaniac of a bird, flew by a couple times with white booty flashing from his beak. He landed in a nearby dying birch tree. Mary took a brief census of the crowd, nodding at most and smiling at all. They were her customers, neighbors, and acquaintances of varying degrees. Only five years sober, Mary had made reconnections, tentatively auditioning her new nondrinking self and fatherless state into a community who had known her otherwise. Five years without drinking was an amazing feat to Mary, but she knew it was nothing in the scheme of a lifetime and was easily squandered. She understood well that the recently sober were not to be trusted because sometimes they puffed out their chests and had the memories of elephants for the follies of others and the memory of a mayfly when it came to their own.

Then Mary experienced a personal miracle. No religious body would have called it a miracle at all, nor would it have miracle status in most minds. They did not have a horse in the race, as Mary's father would have said. A warm hand brushed Mary's forearm. Mary's heart sang "hallelujah." Sadie Barnes stood next to her, and she looked not one iota less beautiful than the first day Mary had met her thirty-seven years in the past.

The news that the Whistler school board had hired a new high school superintendent named Sadie Barnes and that she had lived in Whistler previously had filtered into the General Store. Mary heard Sadie was making trips back and forth between St. Paul, where she had lived, and Whistler. Little by little she was moving her life to Whistler again. It pained Mary that she had heard this news from Mayor Carl rather than from a personal call on her landline, which had had the same number since it was installed over sixty years ago.

She had looked for Sadie. With a mature reserve that surprised Mary herself, she had resisted the temptation to take a position on the roof of her store with binoculars and not move until she saw with her own eyes that Sadie was back. She counted it a miracle that Sadie had come back at all.

Bob's tail wagged. Mary supposed the same would have been true for her if she had a tail. The dog had never met Sadie but had heard about her incessantly after store hours when Mary in drunken crying jags would tell the hound how much she loved and missed Sadie. In sobriety she had told Bob stories about her time with Sadie. She suspected the dog appreciated more the reminiscences that hadn't included vomiting. Nervous anticipation brought an ache to Mary's body. The ache turned to a sharp pain as she beheld her dear, old friend. She wanted to hug Sadie and hold on to her.

Wow, seeing Sadie again and a dead body all in the same day and so close to Carnival. This would be an auspicious summer.

"What do you make of this?" Sadie said like their last conversation hadn't been a fight and occurred more than thirty years earlier. "A dead body is messing up one of your best fishing spots."

Mary didn't miss a beat. She instantly followed Sadie's lead. "I don't know. This spot hasn't been very good in the last few years." She shook her head, sneaking glances at Sadie. "I may need to buy a boat and fish the bigger lakes. And for your information there's two dead bodies."

"No, really?"

Mary scratched the side of her head and tried to sound unaffected by the sudden appearance of Sadie Barnes, but she was shaken. She swallowed so many times her mouth went dry. She raked her hand through her short-cropped gray hair, swept a hand over the front of her shirt to check for crumbs, and stood taller, pulling in a tummy that had come to relax over her waistband like it was smitten with Mary's feet.

She'd just been thinking of this woman a few minutes before and most every day for the past three decades, but as much as Mary had dreamed of being with Sadie again her sudden closeness choked her. Considering all they'd been to each other

Mary thought she should have had fair warning, some visceral siren that signaled Sadie's presence. She expected natural premonitions attuned to the vibrations on the sutures that had held her heart together since it was broken those years ago. She imagined the stitches made of a copolymer, but she thought it would be ironic if it were catgut or simple cotton laced through the chambers of her heart and pulling tighter since Sadie moved away.

"Maybe we've got us a murder."

"Murder? Why'd you say something like that?" Sadie punched Mary's shoulder. "Murder? How could that be? Couldn't it just be an accident? Two dead bodies?" Sadie stood on tiptoes, looking at the scene. "Jesus on a bicycle!"

"Ouch. What?"

Sadie looked flushed. Mary hoped it was because she was standing next to Mary, but she couldn't be sure and she certainly wouldn't ask.

Her head swerved and swayed as Sadie maneuvered for a clearer view. "That sheriff told the coroner that the man from the lake has a bullet hole in his neck. I don't believe it. How on God's green earth? And who is that man on the shore?"

"Can't you just swear properly like the rest of us?" Mary looked at Sadie as she massaged the place where Sadie had hit her. "How do you know all that?"

"Remember, Mary, I read lips."

Sadie had made her declaration as if it had the same authority as asserting she had been a Navy Seal, but Mary didn't challenge her. "You got all that from just lips?" Mary stared at Sadie's lips. There was sarcasm to her tone. Perhaps they both knew it, but Sadie didn't comment. Mary was thankful that Sadie didn't walk away. "Is the school buttoned up for the day or do you have to go back?"

"Not much to do yet. I organized my office. Marvin is buffing the floors. Just like everything else, school year preparations must wait until after the Carnival. I'm done for the day."

Right there. That would have been the time for the new and improved Mary to ask Sadie to join her for a coffee. Mary knew it, but she didn't do it. Fool that she was and had been habitually, she didn't say anything.

Bob nosed Sadie's crotch. She pushed him away gently. "Your dog?"

"Bob, sit." Mary blushed and nodded. "Meet Bob Barker the Sixth."

Sadie laughed. "I see you have continued the Caine family laziness for naming pets."

Mary smiled. "That crow on a limb of the nearest oak tree is named Edwin."

"Oh. After your father?"

"Yep, I call him Win for short. I'm all for recycling."

"How do you know that particular crow is the one you named? Don't they pretty much look alike?"

"Not if you look closely or are another crow. I was a crow in a former life. I think Win and I were related then too. I recognize him more from his crimes and misdemeanors than his appearance."

"What's that bird doing? Is he looking for clues?" Sadie laughed and looked at her watch. "Speaking of mysterious happenings, I'm surprised you're here. It's not even noon. You don't close until seven p.m. Aren't you missing the rush of shoppers? You might miss a few dimes, not that you've ever needed the money."

Mary's stomach clutched. She heard the ridicule in Sadie's tone and knew it was fairly placed. Her interpretation was that Mary's dedication to the store and Whistler was still a sore spot for Sadie and an obvious defect of character in Mary.

"Don't tell me you actually hired someone to help you with the store. That I want to see."

Another jab. "Okay, I won't tell you that." It wouldn't be true anyway. Didn't she know how expensive that would be? Mary ran the store herself. "I'm thinking about hiring on some help." *Am I?* "I'm not getting any younger."

"I guess neither of us is." Sadie looked at Mary.

Mary was again caught off guard by Sadie's eyes that in some light seemed blue and in other light were perfectly and obviously green. "I was surprised to hear you were back." Mary supposed this statement was her own type of counterpunch. She stared straight ahead without peeking to see if the hit had landed.

"I started about a dozen letters to you to let you know I was coming, maybe two dozen. None of them hit the right note."

"The right note, eh?" Mary smiled. "Did they clang and clash?"

"Just like the junior high band! Isn't that what your father would say?"

"Yes, he used that metaphor for about everything that didn't ring true. He probably came up with the comparison from the torture of listening to me practice the cornet when I was a kid. He came to my concerts—a generous word for the racket we made." Mary smiled again, thinking of her father. "Sometimes when he was drinking and in a particularly somber state he'd ask me to play 'Taps' for him."

"Did you play 'Taps' at his actual funeral?"

"Nah, I couldn't have done it. An actual veteran battled the cold April air—he nearly slipped into the grave—before he belted out the tune on the heels of the guns blasting. I still feel the shivers of it."

"That makes sense." Sadie's smile was slight, her eyes compassionate.

It was moments like this when Mary most missed her dad. He would have had words to help her know how to feel and what to say to Sadie. "What would your letter have said? If you don't mind my asking."

"There were many variations. One might have said something like, 'Dear Mary, I'm coming back to Whistler in case you want to brace yourself or your partner.'" Sadie glanced quickly at Mary and then turned away again.

Like I'd take up with someone so soon.

Mary's smile dissolved. Her eyes stung in her head. She blinked rapidly, daring tears to try to pass through the sphincters of her tear ducts. Mouth shut, she breathed through her nose.

Perhaps Sadie noticed. "Well, I better get home to let Muffin out."

"Muffin? Muffin?" Mary slapped her knee.

"Muffin the Fifth I believe. I know. You don't like those food names for dogs. You think it insults their dignity."

"No, I was just surprised that you too seemed to have embraced the Caine family laziness for naming pets. And yes, I do believe pet owners should resist the temptation to name their animals after food."

Before Mary could restate her well-known, impeccably reasoned argument, Sadie added, "Graham named her. Ironic, I suppose. He too was all for recycling and didn't know it."

Graham. That's a conversation killer.

Mary didn't say anything to that. The mention of Sadie's husband, Graham, stopped Mary, stopped her from talking, trying, and hoping. His name was no less a deterrent three years after his death, which Mary had discovered accidently while scanning the *Pioneer Press* obits one Sunday. She risked asking a question rather than crawling under the closest rock. "How is Muffin Number Five?"

"Blind, most days incontinent, won't eat regular dog food, and still bites even though her paws outnumber her teeth." Sadie's expression brightened at the very name of her furry companion.

"So, she's about the same as the original model. Maybe our two dogs could get together, meet, and smell one another sometime."

Sadie laughed. Mary's and Sadie's eyes met, and they smiled at one another in silence.

For Mary, Sadie's face was like sunlight breaking through the clouds. Damn, her eyes were blue. When Sadie laughed, Mary felt like she'd won the lottery. She hoped that in that look they shared, that moment, that everything she felt in her heart was being communicated through her eyes. Because to speak was to open her chest and expose her heart to the elements.

Car doors slammed. The mood and moment were broken. Mary startled. Sadie looked away from Mary and scanned the movements by the downed bodies. Then she leaned in and whispered to Mary, "Do you think that sheriff will tell you anything about this case as it goes along?" She stood upright again and crossed her arms.

"I doubt it. I'm not in his good graces since I shooed Mayor Carl out of the store and posted a sign prohibiting guns in my establishment."

"Mayor Carl. I suppose he still runs things like Whistler is his empire. Does he still wear that fake poppy on his lapel?"

"Yep, Veteran's Day and every other day of the year. That poppy in his lapel is so old, it may be one of the originals from Flanders Field. Earlier in the year he expanded his fashion accessories to include a mother of pearl-handled twenty-two caliber revolver, worn in his waistband." Mary pushed out her middle and patted her stomach.

"He carries it here, in the front of his pants, equal-distance from the red suspenders he wears to keep up his pants and complement his khaki summer suitcoat. He's fatter now, which is good, otherwise he'd probably shoot off his male member." Mary snuck a look at Sadie. She smiled and still seemed interested. "Anyway, back to the disgruntled Sheriff Spelt, he told me I was a fascist and couldn't discriminate against good, red-blooded Americans with a permit to carry. I told him that I too am an American and have good, red blood, but I would prefer to not have any of my blood or that of my neighbors spilt on my floors.

"He said, 'Don't be provoking people, Mary.'" Mary mimicked the sheriff's speech and stance. "'It's not very ladylike and bad for business.' I'd have liked to have brained him right there, but it seemed counterproductive. When I see his big, swollen, tight-skinned fingers pointing at me all I can think is 'cheddar dog.'"

Sadie put her hand over her mouth, covering her laughter. "So, it looks like we aren't going to learn much more than we know already." She again leaned closer and whispered to Mary. "The sheriff, Cheddar Dog, says he thinks it's Buddy Latiskee who they pulled from the lake. I remember the surname, but Buddy doesn't ring any bells. You know him?"

"Not personally. Buddy's the youngest and an unplanned chip off the old block, if gossip is to be believed. I'll be damned. The Royce kid was in my store and thought it was a Latiskee. He didn't know what a Latiskee was, but he was right. What are they saying about the other guy?"

"The sheriff has gloves on and he's looking through the man's suit pockets. Doesn't look like he's finding much."

"It must be someone in sales or soliciting votes—not many people around here dress in suits other than for weddings and funerals."

"You don't suppose?" Sadie mumbled as she kept her eyes on the crime scene briefly and abruptly changed the subject. "I was so sorry to hear about the death of your father."

"I got your card." Mary didn't say that she kept that card and every letter Sadie ever wrote to her in a shoe box beside her bed. The letters were no longer restrained with a blue ribbon. That exercise was empty repetition. She didn't say that sometimes she traced the indention of the pen on paper to feel closer to holding Sadie's hand, her fingers laced between Mary's own.

"Your dad dying, it must have been the saddest day of your life, Mary." Sadie locked eyes with Mary.

"Almost." Mary smiled a sad smile.

"Good to see you, Mary Caine."

"Good to see you, Sadie Barnes."

Sadie touched Mary's arm again and smiled, "In case you haven't heard, I'm back living in my old apartment above the laundromat. Circle of life, huh?"

Mary quickly put her hand over the place Sadie had touched her like she was capturing the gesture to ponder over at another time. "I'd like to hear the other versions of the letter you almost wrote me about coming back here." Mary would have liked to ask Sadie why she hadn't been to the store yet. What was she doing for groceries?

Sadie nodded her head, turned, and walked back toward her apartment. Mary thought to herself that she could have offered to walk back with her or Sadie could have suggested it.

The moment passed, but as Sadie walked across the lake park grounds to the road Mary thought Sadie's butt looked good.

A shiny, new model pickup barreled to a stop behind the coroner's van. A tall, lanky man, older than Mary, hurried out of the driver's seat. Without closing the truck door, he charged over to where the bodies lay. Sheriff Spelt and Dr. Hanson caught him in their arms and kept him from getting to the corpses. A woman followed behind the man. Mary recognized her as Lois Latiskee.

Once the man stopped pushing his way the sheriff talked to him. After a moment or two the sheriff reached down and grasped the corner of the tarp covering the body that had been in the water.

The crowd of people Mary had been a part of fell silent— so silent it was like they sucked the sounds exchanged like a parabolic microphone. Mary heard the sheriff say, "I'm going to lift the tarp and you can look at him. You can't touch him. I will tackle you if you try."

Martin Latiskee nodded his assent to the sheriff's terms.

Sheriff Spelt lifted the tarp.

Martin and Lois's keening filled the air and enveloped the ground with a realism that spread like a pandemic disease through the gathering. Anyone who had lost someone they loved knew at least a fraction of the sorrow those parents felt. They'd lost a child and maybe grandchildren they'd never hold and see in their young faces the likeness of Lloyd. Martin folded Lois into his arms like he was a giant insect and she was his second set of wings. They cried and rocked. The sheriff replaced the tarp and stood between it and the parents.

As quickly as they swept onto the lakeshore, the Latiskees got back in their truck and drove recklessly out away from the boat landing, leaving ruts in the grass from their spinning tires. These marks would be excused.

The crowd dispersed soundlessly. People brushed past, littering more nods, but no words. There were no words.

Mary stood in place facing upstream, staring at the spot where the bodies had been. She treaded water there until all but a few stragglers had gone on their way. She wished she'd had the courage to approach Lois Latiskee, touch her arm, or offer some expression of compassion. She hadn't and that moment had passed.

She imagined most of the crowd would speculate about the event in a place that offered beer on tap and roasted chicken. The communal watering hole was a natural attraction. Mary didn't swallow her grief with beer anymore, but she'd welcome a large bowl of potatoes with poultry gravy if it were offered to her.

Win swooped close to Mary's head before flying high away from the lake. Again, he had something hanging from his crow face, which reminded Mary she hadn't checked his cache in the backroom of the store lately. That hiding spot was in her building, and Mary felt an obligation to inventory what the salvaging, thieving bird had collected. Not that he had filched anything of value so far.

"If you and your fine hound are here, how am I supposed to pick up hamburger buns and eggs at your store?" Joey Kay's face was all smile as he cocked his head to the side looking at Mary. Joey owned one of only two gas and service stations in town. He performed much of the service work on the older model cars in Whistler. That meant he knew Mary's thirdhand truck intimately. He carried himself like a man who knew the secrets of the world. In Mary's mind he knew the most important ones and shared them liberally.

"Walk along with me, Joey. I'll open the store up for you. I'll find you the freshest buns and eggs and throw in a small roast I have been saving for you and some peas." Mary motioned toward the coroner van crunching gravel until it moved silently onto the blacktop. "Crazy business this."

"Lloyd Buddy Latiskee—he drove an older model Dodge. You saw his parents, Martin and Lois there. They don't come to town much. I can only imagine how heartbroken they are, just like any of us would be. Damn shame to bury your child."

"I thought I recognized one of them living in town," Mary said. "That surprised me. I thought they either stayed at home or flew the coop entirely."

"I guess you could say Buddy flew away, at least his soul did." Joey walked along with Mary back to the store. Bob Barker followed along behind, still intent on pissing every few yards. Joey waited as Mary unlocked the door of the General Store and flipped on the lights. Win slipped in ahead of everyone and returned to his cage. Bob Barker went to his spot and harrumphed on the floor like the whole trip had been enormously wearing and boring.

"Appreciate you reopening for me. I don't know how I would have explained to Carolyn that I forgot the only things she put on the grocery list this morning."

"I suppose you were surprised the store was closed?" Mary bowed to her reputation for squeezing as many sales out of a day as possible.

"Didn't surprise me a bit," Joey said. "I know your concern for this town and all its people."

If he had said she were the smartest or loveliest person in the world it would not have meant as much as what he had just said.

She stood taller. "You know anything about the other guy?"

Joey removed his Conoco cap, wiped across his brow with his forearm. "No clue. I heard he didn't have any identification which is strange."

"Hmm, I guess he was robbed too."

Joey leaned in as if to whisper but spoke at normal volume. "Apparently, the sheriff has some concerns this could be the start of a serial murder spree and he is questioning whether the Carnival should go off as usual. You know, he's wondering if it is wise to invite so many extra people to town?"

Mary swatted at the notion as if it were a mosquito. "Serial killer? Cancel the Carnival? Does that sound as dumb to you as it does to me?"

"Maybe the sheriff has been watching too much Netflix."

"Or worse, he hates the Carnival. He'll be hung for treason." Mary grabbed a can of Diet Mountain Dew from the cooler and took her place behind the counter.

"I have to admit the discovery of two dead people gives me the willies." Joey clutched the brown paper sack of groceries to his chest. "See you at the meeting Saturday?"

Mary nodded affirmatively. All the affection she'd ever felt for Joey had grown exponentially when he led her into recovery. She saw him every week at her Saturday morning AA meeting in Big Falls and she called him or went to his gas station any time she was tempted to drink again.

Joey left the store. Now that it was open again it gradually filled with people acting like they had newly discovered needs. They came solo and in small clutches. Most talked about the bodies if they knew about them. This contagion moved through the store so that Mary was certain no one left the store without contact.

Many people glanced at the quote of day and weekly specials posted on a wall Mary'd painted with blackboard paint. The surface area had gradually increased as the months went by and Mary thought of more things she wanted to post there. Some people left messages on the board for the community as a whole or for specific individuals. Mary only lightly censored the messages, erasing profanity and poorly drawn genitalia. She surveyed the shoppers and other beings in the store.

Bob Barker, Win, and Vanna White were in their respective places. Both Protestant ministers came in the store at the same time. Mary wondered if either were headed out to the Latiskee home? She was relieved they didn't offer up any platitudes about the larger meaning of the deaths. Instead, they jabbered in the bread aisle, ignoring the priest, who had coincidentally discovered an urgent need for bread.

"The high fiber loaves are on sale," Mary announced in their general direction. *God bless them, they all three could use as much fiber as they could stomach.*

Each of clergy had greeted Mary and said they hoped to see her on Sunday. In turn, to each one Mary said, "See you at church. Sit by the window."

June from the post office took a cart back to the hardware section. Judy and Blanch Reeves picked over the summer sale table piled high with bug dope, charcoal, fishing supplies, and s'mores fixings. They each absentmindedly petted Vanna White, who lounged nearby. This burble of trade continued all afternoon into the early evening. Mary's smile widened as her cash take swelled. She refilled her diminishing stock on the shelves, making trip after trip to the backroom to keep up with product her neighbors needed that particular day. She enjoyed the influx of cash, but she grew tired and frustrated that she didn't learn any verifiable information about the threat to cancel the Carnival or the suspicious deaths.

CHAPTER FOUR

I Am Not Alone in the World

During the waning minutes before closing Mary restocked the candy and pop and fluffed the clearance table with a few more items she had discounted for quick sale, but her mind was on Sadie Barnes. Forget it being the unsavory business of dead bodies that brought her directly into Mary's orbit again. Mary was grateful that Sadie had returned to Whistler. That unexpected homecoming got her thinking and, more dangerously, it propelled her down the slippery slope of remembering.

Sadie had moved to Whistler right out of college to take her first teaching job as Whistler's high school English teacher. Mary too had just completed a college degree from a state school program in religious studies with a minor in biology and had returned to Whistler to run the family store with her father. Mary had briefly entertained the idea of pursuing graduate school, but college life had been a tumultuous time for her. When she wasn't studying, she was building up her tolerance for alcohol, warding off unwelcome attention from men, and wondering what in the hell to do with her attraction to women.

That didn't go away by prayer or promises and appeared to be a chronic, irreversible condition.

Then Mary met Sadie Barnes. Suddenly, everything made sense. It was quantum physics, DNA, evolution, and the Big Bang Theory all in one. Loving women was a natural state of being, not a viral persistent rash. She didn't need treatment, new distractions, an exorcism. She needed to meet her people. She wasn't alone in the world and it was even possible she could have someone to love and maybe, just maybe, someone could love her back. Her dad had said there was a "cover for every pot." That was good news to Mary because most days she felt like she had no lid or had flipped her own.

That day, when Sadie first entered Mary's life, Mary had been on her knees on the floor of the store. She'd looked up after she'd spilled a small box of ball bearings. Sadie came through the door moving so fast she almost tripped over Mary.

Sadie, who appeared already winded, got her balance just long enough to lose her footing by stepping on a bearing. She crashed to her bottom on the wooden floor in front of Mary like she'd been dropped from the sky. They were eye-to-eye, only inches apart. Mary thought she smelled fruit trees, heard birds singing, and that she could die having finally glimpsed the face of God. No wonder Mary had been in prayer position.

"Jesus riding shotgun, everybody I ask about where to buy things for my new apartment says go to Caine's General Store." Sadie rubbed her backside as she smiled at Mary.

"The bigger ticket and more sophisticated items like appliances and electronics are sold at Rahn's Hardware, kitty-corner across the street. We carry groceries and sundry household supplies."

"I don't suppose you also repair broken tailbones?"

"Not on Saturdays," Mary said. She touched her hair, hoping it wasn't sticking out all over, which was a fine enough 'do for working at the store, but certainly not right for this introduction. She looked down at her clothes. They were clean and her shirt buttoned on the appropriate side. She was dressed as a woman, not like the son her father had never had.

"I hope you don't mind, but I parked my dog, Muffin, outside tied to your bench."

"Tying him there is fine, but you should probably apologize to him for that name."

Once she was upright again, Mary looked out the window and spied a little black and white dog with unruly, wiry hair, and tiny ears. Mary looked at Sadie—a short-haired petite woman with gleaming chestnut hair, arresting blue eyes, and tiny ears.

She offered her hand to Sadie and helped her to her feet. "Excepting the risk of injury, this is the place in Whistler where people come for most everything. We have wingnuts to walnuts to whiskey; herring to hairbrushes to hair remover; things to satisfy your sweet tooth, sweaty feet, or Swedish grandma; tanning butter to almond butter; rakes, shovels, and hoes, swing sets, bikes, and ski poles." Mary lowered her head but raised her eyes. "Shall I go on?" It was a litany she'd heard her father say nearly every day they'd had the store. She waited in anticipation to know if it sounded clever or odd to Sadie.

"You sound like Yukon Cornelius in 'Rudolph the Red-Nosed Reindeer,'" Sadie remarked.

Then in unison they said, "Cornmeal and gun powder and ham hocks and guitar strings!"

"Tell me what you need for your apartment?" Mary grabbed a shopping cart.

"What I don't need is probably the shorter list. It's furnished, you know, and above the laundromat. It's like having in-floor heating, which will be nice in winter, but in summer feels like I'm in an upper duplex in h-e-double toothpick." Sadie covered her mouth with her hand. "Oops, I hope my cussing didn't offend you."

"No, I enjoy cussing for the most part. You should meet my dad. He doesn't swear as much now, but for the first few years of my life I thought 'goddamned' was as common an adjective as 'red' or 'big.'"

Sadie glanced at a list she carried. "I need personal things and practical things besides groceries, of course. Do you really have towels?"

"Do we have towels? My dad would say we have both bath and kitchen towels, painting trowels, and remedies for your bowels."

"I'll stick with kitchen towels for now." Sadie stuffed her canvas shopping bags into the child seat section of the large, metal shopping cart Mary had pulled loose from the line of entangled cages. Up and down all four aisles Sadie pushed the cart and filled it with household linens, cleaners, food storage wraps, glass containers, bottled water, and about two dozen frozen dinners. She must have noticed a sour look on Mary's face as Mary gaped at the mountain of boxed dinners.

Sadie picked up one of the dinners. She pointed to the picture of chicken, corn, and potatoes on the box. "There's a microwave, you see, and I'm not much of a cook. I'd rather read than cook or bake."

"I'd rather read than cook too, but I'd read less or faster rather than live on these dinners. The portions are miniscule and the sodium is very high." Mary keyed the prices into the cash register and loaded the items into her bags.

"Well," Sadie's face bloomed red, "not all of us cook, bake, and sew. You may not have heard, but women have the vote, own property. A woman is allowed a large continuum of interests!"

"The Nineteenth Amendment, I am aware." Mary noted the agitation and surmised that Sadie had given that speech before. Sadie paid, returned the cart, lugged her grocery bags to her side, and started for the door, singing several more verses. "Did you know that Finland, Australia, Denmark, Norway, Canada, Germany, Poland, and even Russia gave women the vote before the US? France was even later to the party than America."

"Miss, I have no expectations that you cook, bake, or sew any more than I expect you to place in the Kentucky Derby. My criticism of those frozen dinners was a poor excuse and attempt of an introduction and an offer to have you join my father and me for dinner. You can bring Muffin. I promise not to eat him."

Sadie lowered her eyes briefly and blew out air like it leaked away from a wilting balloon. "I'm sorry. My name is Sadie Barnes, the new English teacher." She set one of the shopping bags on the floor and put out her hand to Mary.

"Hello, Sadie, I'm Mary Caine, the former and future grocer's assistant to my father, who owns and runs this store. Normally, he is underfoot except for right this minute when he's suspiciously absent. He's probably off somewhere reading or drinking beer or both." Mary took Sadie's hand and held it.

"Pleased to meet you. We live upstairs. After hours, you enter from outside in the back. Tonight, we're having Crockpot beef roast, carrots, onions, potatoes, and for dessert, French apple pie à la mode minus the French apple pie. Too hot to bake pies and there are no decent pie recipes for the slow cooker. Tomorrow night is honey-glazed chicken thighs, garlic mashed potatoes, and corn. If I feel inspired, I will be serving a poor man's version of key lime pie. Tonight or tomorrow night—dinner's at six thirty p.m. Come to either or neither, but I hope you will come to both. I think we have most everything you need to make a good home here in Whistler."

"Half past six, beef roast. Can I bring anything?"

Mary reached over the counter to where she kept a galvanized pail of fresh flower bouquets. Some of the flowers she'd grown herself in a measly garden alongside the parking lot, but most she purchased from other more prolific gardeners. She lifted the biggest arrangement out of the pail, shook the water off the bouquet's neatly trimmed, banded stems, and slipped the flowers into an opening in Sadie's grocery bag.

"There, bring flowers for the table."

"They're lovely." Sadie leaned her face into the blooms. "I'll be there!" She left the store.

Mary watched as Sadie retreated down the steps, untied Muffin, and proceeded down the sidewalk with shopping bags in both hands. At that moment, Mary's dad stepped up behind her and put his hand on her shoulder. Mary jumped and nearly threw an elbow into him.

He'd apparently heard the whole exchange. "You think that one is a keeper?"

"I don't know, Dad. She's big enough, but it's not like I can tell too much from that brief encounter." Mary didn't disclose that she was already in love with Sadie. "Pardon the mixed metaphor, but it's not like I'm picking out a melon."

"No, of course not. You wouldn't want to thump her. It's more like peaches—a sniff and a gentle squeeze would tell you a lot."

"Or get me slapped and arrested."

Her father winked at her and then took up the wholesale order sheet from behind the counter. "I think I can save us two cents a can on soup if I use this other distributor."

Mary grew embarrassed every time her father said something about other women and their suitability for Mary. It wasn't that she was ungrateful her father accepted she was lesbian, but sometimes it seemed he wouldn't shut up about it—like he was atoning for a previous phobia or hate crime. He looked out for potential dating material, commented, and advised Mary on romantic entanglements without her invitation. Just once, Mary wanted him to wait for her solicitation. Besides, he couldn't claim any specialty in relationships. His wife had left him.

It was not lost on Mary that her father's interest in Sadie was not solely about pairing Mary up with a like-spirited woman. She knew her father sought the secondary gain of having a new dinner and debate partner. He'd exhausted the usual suspects and irritated most of the good brains in town, including Mary, with his hypothetical questions and scenarios that were amusing until he was drunk and irritable and critical of the guest's replies. Mary could name at least four people in town who had stopped talking to her father altogether because of an argument about what pigs would eat.

Along came Sadie, a fresh college graduate who majored in English and education, the perfect complement for his unused major in literature and overused minor in excessive drinking. Mary hoped he could behave himself, doubted he would, and loved him just the same.

CHAPTER FIVE

Guess Who's Coming to Dinner

Lovely Sadie, fresh-minded Sadie arrived for dinner at Mary and her father's apartment above the store promptly at 6:30 p.m. of the day they'd met. Sadie had the bouquet of flowers in tow—the plastic removed and replaced with an orange gingham ribbon. Beside her was Muffin. Mary thought Sadie looked even more beautiful than her memory of her earlier that day. She wished she could take Sadie's picture or paint her portrait so she would always have her face at the ready should she ever require resuscitation.

Mary watched as Sadie eyed the table. Of course, she had noticed the extra place setting. *Oh God, is it too late to crawl into one of the closets or lower cabinets?*

"I see four place settings. Where would you like me to sit? Are you expecting another guest?"

If only it were so simple.

"No, that setting is always there." Ed gestured to a chair on his left for Sadie to seat herself. He pointed to the place setting at the other end of the table. "That setting is for God."

Mary sighed and fidgeted as she took her seat to the right of her father.

"You set a place for God?" Sadie opened her eyes more. A hint of a smile played on her lips.

"It started out as a place setting for Mary's mother in hopes she would rejoin our merry band of ruffians. Some restless, anticipatory months passed, followed by many painful years. Then one day I read a study on the Old Testament book of Jeremiah and the theologian—a Peterson, I believe—likened prayer time to an intimate dinner with God. I liked the image and I've left the place setting on the table for God or Andrea, whoever first attends that intimate dinner. I am not embarrassed to say I am a man who prays and drinks." He flipped the tab of another beer, his third since the store closed by Mary's count. He offered one to Sadie. She declined.

Uh-oh.

Mary bristled but watched intently. Back then, she'd wished she'd had the good sense to slam a couple beers herself before dinner to quiet her nerves. She hadn't been certain if drinking was a misstep for the occasion. Her father saw all occasions as good times to drink. His missteps would invariably come later.

Did Sadie want to run from the dinner? That's what Mary wondered and worried over. But Sadie remained seated. She unfurled her cloth napkin and smoothed it on her lap. "I believe in prayer too, Mr. Caine, although I must admit I'm prone to arguing with God most of the time."

"Me too." He poured water into Sadie's glass.

Muffin circled. Her nails clicked on the hardwood floors until she finally perched below Sadie's chair. Bob Barker had already examined her stem to stern with his nose. He left her and reclined in his place across the room. Mary relaxed a bit, but then her father wasted no time in starting a game with Sadie Barnes.

"Tell me, Ms. Barnes."

"Please call me, Sadie, Mr. Caine."

"Thank you and please call me Ed." He looked toward the ceiling as if he were creating a line of inquiry but followed with a tried-and-true quandary he had laid before plenty of other dinner guests. "If you were on a deserted island, what one book would you want with you?"

"Wow, I haven't tackled this question since my college freshman seminar, but I love the exercise. My two favorite novels are Elizabeth Strout's *Olive Kitteridge* and Kent Haruf's *Plainsong*, but I don't know that my favorite books are my first choice in this situation. Maybe I should choose something that I've struggled to read or intended to read, but never got to, like Proust or Henry James. Or Shakespeare for that matter. I had to read the bard, but I don't know that I liked or understood much of him." Sadie sucked on her lower lip as she looked at the ceiling, pondering his question. "No, I wouldn't chance being on an island with only Henry James. What if I got frustrated and used *The Golden Bowl* as kindling or *The Ambassadors* as toilet paper? I'd have nothing left to read. Not having something to read would feel like being exiled in purgatory or worse."

The food was on the table being kept warm in the slow cooker, but Mary wished her dad would hurry up and carve the roast and begin serving. Mary was poised for her role in spooning the tender vegetables into serving bowls.

"I suppose that my answer depends on my purpose and circumstances on the island. Am I there alone for the rest of my days? Am I there with possibility of others and the potential of building a community? Should I realistically expect rescue?"

Mary felt some indigestion despite her empty stomach. Already Mary's dad had Sadie talking about repopulating the earth from a desert island. For a moment Mary allowed herself to imagine being on that island with Sadie. She pictured a blue lagoon and a sandy beach. She pinched herself on the leg. She was being just as forward as her father. To Mary, the conversation was indecent, but it held her attention like she would learn something very important if she listened.

Her father smiled with glee and put his large hands together like he might applaud. "How would those circumstances differ in your mind, Sadie?" Ed stood, speared the roast from the slow cooker, and placed it on a platter to slice.

It's about time.

Mary stood beside him as she ladled vegetables from the Crock-pot into serving bowls.

"Well, if I was on a deserted island without hope of rescue or other companionship"—she glanced at Mary—"I would want the collected works of John Steinbeck. Is it cheating to ask for the collected works? Almost everybody has a one-volume collected works on Amazon."

"Yes, yes, fine choice." Ed lowered his head and peered at Sadie carefully. "Not the Bible?" Ed continued the game.

"I could live with the Bible just fine. I know it pretty well, believe it or not. I appreciate the stories, poetry, law, and proverbs, but I don't believe I'm obligated to choose it as my one and only book. No offense intended." She glanced back and forth between Mary and Ed. "I mean, you set a place setting for God. It seems safe to assume you are a religious people."

"I wouldn't call us religious people. Would you, Mary?" He looked at Mary but didn't wait for a reply before he turned again to Sadie. "Mary and I read from the major religions, post quotes on the blackboard in the store for the edification of our friends and neighbors, and attend the services of all three formal congregations in town on a rotation basis."

"Rotation? What, like a volleyball team or bullpen?"

This wasn't the first time Mary had felt embarrassed by the theory and resulting habit she shared with her quixotic father.

"Certainly, you'd agree that each church has its strengths." Ed sat back in his chair and let his fingers do sort of meditative push-ups against each other—a thinking pose. "I like the Catholic Church for its music, majesty, and the practice of confession. The Bible Church far and away has the best social justice sermons, and the Lutherans have the best lefse dinner, and I love the fragrance of lilies when they line the cross at Easter." Ed smiled with perfect teeth, sat forward, took his can of beer, drained it, and opened another. "And no matter their particular theology they all need to buy groceries to eat."

"So, you and Mary attend a different church each week. What about the fourth Sunday or those months when there are five?"

"We take those Sundays for ourselves," Mary said. "Dad calls those days our time for attending 'Bedside Baptist.'"

"So, you'd take Steinbeck if you were alone. And if you were building a society?" Ed asked as he layered two generous pieces of perfectly marbled beef roast on Sadie's plate.

"Then I'd insist on more than one book." Sadie slathered the meat with gravy. She added a generous dollop of butter to the vegetables Mary served her. Mary was impressed.

"You like to stretch the rules of this inquiry, I see." Ed looked at Sadie over the top of his glasses and then turned to Mary and grinned.

"I suspect that I will break many rules before I leave this town." Sadie smiled. She sipped her water.

Mary hoped Sadie was right and that they would break several rules together. She fell more deeply in love like love was a cavern leading to the center of the earth.

Sadie continued with a strong, resolute tone and elevated volume. "I must stretch the rules in this instance. The civilization of a nation is at risk." She tasted a sliver of potato and waved her fork in the air. "Mary, I may never be able to stomach a frozen dinner again. How did you learn to cook like this?"

"I blame him mostly." Mary pointed her fork toward her dad. "If I hadn't learned after my mother left, we would have starved—ironic given our vocation. Although I'm not above watching a cooking show as I listen to the baseball game on the radio."

"Yankees fan, are you?" Sadie continued eating.

"Excuse me?" Mary nearly choked at the suggestion. "We haven't known each other long, but what would possibly cause you to peg me as a Yankees fan? I am a Minnesota Twins fan through and through."

"I was teasing about the Yankees, but I'm serious about your cooking. Blame or credit, I thank whatever person or impulse caused you to cook so gloriously. This meal is delicious." Sadie closed her eyes as she chewed.

"My daughter cooks like her mother did." He took a long pull on his beer and set the can back down on the table. "She cooks as if love were an ingredient stored in the cupboard or

refrigerator and could be spooned or sifted into every recipe."
He swiped his hands together. "Chop, chop. Are you delaying
your answer, Sadie?"

"I have no need to delay, Ed. I can think of no less than a
dozen books that should be allowed on that island along with
another hundred blank ones for this new nation to write. What
happened to Mrs. Caine?"

"Buried in the basement, guarded by alligators." He swatted
away the question.

"Dad, that's not funny."

"You are right, Mary. It's not funny at all. There are no
alligators." He turned from Mary to Sadie. "The truth is much
worse. She joined the circus, but that's a tale for another day.
Back to our inquiry. Name three books." Ed sat down to his
dinner, pushed his can of beer to the side, filled a glass with
water, but he barely took his eyes off Sadie.

Mary wanted to kick her dad under the table but restrained
herself because another part of her was so very sorry for his
sadness since her mom left. Still, she was also proud of his mind
and unwavering dedication to any debate.

"You strike a hard bargain." Sadie took a fork of potatoes and
gravy into her mouth, closed her eyes, and then leaned toward
Mary. When she opened her eyes she said, "I'm fortunate to be
strengthened by such lovely food. I'd insist on a good history
book. I'd choose Howard Zinn's *A People's History of the United
States*. The Constitution and Bill of Rights, most certainly, but
what should I use to model fiction and poetry with only one
choice for a whole nation? Dickens!" Her eyes sparkled like she
had a solved a math theorem. "The collected works of Charles
Dickens would at least provide humor, good storytelling, and
creative use of language. There, I stand by my answer. I hope
you don't mind that I didn't choose an American writer." She
tucked into her roast beef.

Of course, Mary was looking at her dad wondering if he
found Sadie as unquestionably charming as she did. He smiled
at Sadie, then at Mary, blinked his eyes as he nodded, and turned
back to Sadie. He raised his water glass. "I hope you will grace

our table with your fine mind and beautiful deportment for years to come. Welcome to Whistler."

Bob Barker barked and howled as if startled from a dream or adding his assent. Muffin yipped.

As Mary walked Sadie home that first night under the ruse that she needed one of the large washing machines to clean a comforter—Sadie lived above the laundromat—they talked about the evening and Mary's hope that Sadie would join her and her dad again the next night.

Sadie walked with her hands behind her back, her fingers laced. She hesitated. "You know that I find your father very interesting, so intelligent and courteous, but I hope I haven't given him the impression that I am available for a dating relationship."

"God, no. Why he's old enough to be your father too. He wasn't flirting with you for himself."

"That's a relief." She began walking again, swinging her arms at her sides. "I hope I haven't embarrassed myself by asking that question."

"Not at all. I'm a big fan of clarifications. Dad was being his most amusing self in hopes you'd date me."

"Oh." Sadie looked straight ahead.

Mary couldn't read Sadie's tone or facial expression. She had no idea how Sadie would respond to that disclosure and if she'd thought it through then she'd likely have lost the nerve to say it.

Hurray for the stupidity of youth.

"What did happen to your mother?"

"Truly, she's not buried in the basement. I checked. And there are no alligators. I was very young, only six, but she left us. Dad said that she had a deep calling that apparently summoned her away."

"That's so sad." Sadie stopped in her tracks, looked as though she might cry, and slowly said her next words as if she had chosen them very carefully and they must only be uttered from a stationary position. "I would like to think that I would never be a person who would leave someone I loved, but I guess none of us knows what we would do in every situation." Sadie walked on again.

"I don't know what called her away, but I still expect her to come back. Especially at our Midsummer Carnival time I watch for her. Does that sound weird? It's probably childish."

"Oh no, Mary," Sadie turned to her and touched her shoulder, "having hope is the most mature attitude." A silence hung in the air between them. Mary found it fitting like the pause before or after prayer. They had arrived at the door of Sadie's apartment.

Mary wished Sadie's apartment had been in the next town over so their walk would take all night.

"Well, this is my stop. I guess I'll see you tomorrow night for chicken." Sadie and Muffin went upstairs to the apartment and Mary washed an already clean comforter in the jumbo washer.

Those meals above the store were remarkable, and Mary would have been lying if she didn't admit she had scoured cookbooks and cooking channels for recipes she thought would delight Sadie. But they weren't the meals that stuck in Mary's head. It was the night she and Sadie shared barbequed chicken at the Midsummer Carnival that made Mary swoon with hope, love, and a heavy helping of lust.

She and Sadie had sat in the shade of the band pavilion. There wouldn't be music until later in the evening when the Johnny Holm Band would take the stage, but the ambient sounds of the carnival, bingo calling, the cheerful music of the kiddie rides, laughter and jubilant screams from the riders on the Octopus, Scrambler, and Ferris wheel were enough of a soundtrack for Mary.

Sadie shook her head with her eyes closed. "This is the best barbeque sauce I've ever tasted. Not too sweet, not vinegary."

"My father has seen the recipe, but if he told it to you he'd have to kill you."

"I'd die happy. Who am I kidding? I don't cook. You'd have to cook for me. Would you do that, Mary Caine?" Sadie's enthusiasm shown all over her face and hands. The thick tangy sauce looked like parentheses around her smile. Their eyes locked as Mary reached over, cupped Sadie's jaw in her hand, and with her thumb wiped sauce away from Sadie's face. Mary licked the sauce from her finger and repeated the ablution on the other side of Sadie's face. No words, just that drinking in of each other and the lick of fingers. The world fell silent for Mary. She had no doubt in her mind that she loved Sadie Barnes. She would gladly cook for this woman. She would do anything in the world for this woman.

CHAPTER SIX

Cheddar Dog Finds a Clue

The sweet memory from Mary's first Midsummer Carnival with Sadie Barnes was interrupted by Sheriff Spelt, of all people. Mary started when she noticed him. She hadn't heard the bell on her door jingle, but there he stood like a sentinel at Mary's counter. He was dressed in his drab brown uniform and that oversized Mountie hat—probably made of felted beaver fur and stiff enough to hold water.

Mary stood silent for as long as she could stand it, which wasn't long. "Well, what do you want, Sheriff?"

"I didn't want to interrupt. You seemed deep in thought." His voice and face suggested both the anguish of chronic constipation and an unfamiliarity with the condition of the deep thought he mentioned.

"I was, but I'm back on the surface with you. What is it you need, Sheriff?"

He looked around the store like he was checking for listening ears. "Well, you probably heard there's been two bodies found." He pointed at the shelf behind Mary. "Give me one of those Slim Jims."

"Yep." Mary slipped a greasy, packaged sausage on the counter and rang it into the register. "Buddy Latiskee shot in the throat and some John Doe. I'm not certain of the method of his demise."

He scrutinized Mary then. She wasn't sure if her knowing that much information put her in the category of witch, suspect, or both.

"Don't worry, Sheriff. I didn't shoot Buddy. You may remember, I don't like guns. I don't own one. I'm categorically against killing others. I don't know the other guy. I got my particulars the old-fashioned Whistler way—by gossip and pure speculation."

"Well, keep it under your hat."

Mary took a cap from the selection she sold and put it on her head. It read, "Jesus Is Coming. Look Busy!"

Sheriff Spelt scowled. "Deputy Hart is out at the Latiskee place right now questioning them about Buddy and of course their whereabouts."

"Lucky her." Mary returned the hat to the display area. "I heard Martin Latiskee shoots at people who show up at his place unannounced."

"That's just an old wives' tale."

"Why do they call something an old wives' tale when it's usually the husbands who spread it? And why isn't it a young wives' tale?"

"You are an odd sort of woman, Mary Caine." The sheriff chuckled, coughed, and continued his gesticulations. "Dotty at my office ran the plates of a strange Oldsmobile someone noticed parked a block from the lake. You ever meet him, young Latiskee?"

Mary was about to deny it when her brain clicked. "I think I did. I think Lloyd was in my store last Monday, I believe."

"Why do you remember that?"

"Because it was the day I changed the window display from early days of summer sale generally to get this gardening, Easter, and Memorial Day shit out of the way specifically. I was knee deep in pots, garden gloves, soil mixes, miniature flags, and tacky lawn ornaments. Which reminds me I have squirrel tableau that would perfectly match your uniform." Mary noted the sheriff didn't seem interested in art. "Anyway, he bought my last package of those awful diabetic coma-inducing Peeps and few other palatable groceries. He asked me whether I had any carpentry work for hire."

"Is that a fact?"

"Yes, it is." Mary leaned forward and whispered, "There's been quite a lot of that grocery-buying kind of activity here at the store." She leaned back. "Anyway, I started to tell him about my roof garden project and how I planned to begin it after Carnival. He didn't seem interested. He was probably too expensive anyway."

The sheriff's big head rocked gently on his shoulders as he sucked in his cheeks and squinted at Mary. "I'll tell you one thing. This may be my first murder, but I'm going to solve this case. I'm going to find whoever killed Buddy Latiskee and that Doe guy and they're going to jail for a very long time, no matter what excuse they make up. I just hope I can find the culprit before the next body falls." He sighed, snatched up his Slim Jim, and puffed out his chest, but his belly was still far ahead.

"You're an inspiration. So there's no reason this event should mess with the Carnival?"

"Carnival, Carnival, Carnival. I'm sick of the subject. Nothing but trouble. Me and the other deputies will be putting in long hours doing what? I'll tell you. We'll be babysitting drunks and pot-smoking, horny teenagers."

"At least they'll all be in one spot."

He waved his hand dismissively at Mary. "I don't give diddly-squat whether that carnival ever happens again."

His statement irked Mary, but she supposed he had his reasons. "Anything else you need? Hemorrhoid cream? Breath mints? I was about to lock up after I finish this crossword puzzle." She looked up at Win. "Win, seven letters, another name for stupid, starts with s."

Win chuckled.

Sheriff Spelt dropped a dollar and some change on the counter. "Why do you ask that flying rodent the answers to your puzzle?"

"Crows aren't flying rodents. Pigeons are flying rodents." She regarded Win first and then the sheriff. "You see, Sheriff, I ask Win because the dog can't spell worth crap and my cat won't tell me."

Sheriff Spelt waved her off for a second time. "Has to be a health code violation having these vermin in a grocery store."

As the sheriff turned to leave Win made a ruckus in his cage, flew out, and dropped something on the counter, just missing the sheriff's head.

"What in the hell?"

Mary and the sheriff looked at one another like somebody had farted. Then they examined the square, black thing on the counter.

"What's that?" The sheriff leaned forward, inspecting the droppings.

"I don't know."

Neither of them touched it like it might yet explode.

"Where did it come from?"

"My crow, Win, but I don't know where it was before he got his thieving beak on it."

Sheriff Spelt leaned in closer, backed up again, and squinted at Mary. "Looks like a man's wallet. Are you sure you don't know where this came from?"

"Well, I think it is safe to say that Win found it someplace."

Sheriff Spelt merely nodded. "Right."

"He has a habit of picking up things, mostly pop tops and twist ties, an occasional hair ornament." She felt defensive and embarrassed explaining herself or Win to the sheriff, but she guessed she had obligation since Win was her bird. "I taught my bird to repeat a few words. It's not like I taught him to pick pockets. Besides it looks all wet."

"Give me that pen."

Mary handed a pen to the sheriff and immediately discerned his intention and surprising attention to potential evidence. Without touching it with any part of his hands, he flipped open the wallet.

"Give me a tissue or something." He held his open hand out.

Like an assisting surgical nurse, Mary retrieved supplies for the sheriff, understanding the drill and staying just a step ahead. She hustled to Aisle Two and grabbed a box of quart-size ziplock baggies, a roll of paper towels, and a metal tweezer. She held a baggie open for each thing the sheriff extracted.

"Well, I'll be a monkey's uncle."

Mary thought he was more of a horse's ass but she didn't correct him.

"This wallet belongs to someone from Bloomington. McConnell Kavanaugh." Using the tweezer, he held the license up to the light and scrutinized the thumb-sized picture. A smile broke open his puffy face. "I believe I know just where to return Mr. Kavanaugh's wallet, although he won't be needing it much in the morgue in Big Falls. The dead man is McConnell Kavanaugh."

Sheriff Spelt dropped the driver's license in the baggie and fished out an employee identification card. "Same name. He works, worked for Big Bottom Foods."

"Odd, I wonder what brought Big Bottom to town?" Mary said.

"That Oldsmobile of course." The sheriff stuffed the wallet into its own baggie, gathered the bags, and started out of the store. He stopped, looked up at Win who was back in his cage, and then at Mary. "You and I are going to have to have another discussion on how that bird came into possession of the wallet of a dead stranger."

"He's not a stranger anymore. You know his name, address, weight, and organ donor status. As for Win, you can mirandize him and ask him anything. He's a bird of few words, but I've never known him to lie for the most part."

Sheriff Spelt looked at Win. "Don't leave town." He left the store.

Mary locked the door after him. Before she turned off the lights in the front of the store she eyed Win. "How did you get a wallet? Big Bottom Foods? Really?" Big Bottom Foods was a behemoth food wholesaler. Their branding included a wide-bottomed housewife in fifties hairstyle and apron gazing into an open refrigerator stuffed to the gills with fresh meat, dairy, and produce. The logo read, "Big Bottom Foods: feeding a great nation one family at a time."

She looked up at Win again. "What have you gotten yourself into? More importantly, what have you gotten me into?"

Win remained silent.

"Pleading the fifth, I see."

He preened himself since he lacked a mate to assist him. Mary knew the feeling. She had the same vacancy. She walked slowly to the back of the store shaking her head, turned off the remaining first-floor lights, and climbed the stairs to her apartment. Bob Barker followed along behind her.

CHAPTER SEVEN

The Boy

The next day Mary dragged through her personal morning rituals and the store opening routine. The quote for the day was a long one: "Non-violence means avoiding not only external physical violence but also internal violence of spirit. You not only refuse to shoot a man, but you refuse to hate him."—Written by Martin Luther King, Jr.

She was tired from the inordinate level of sales and stocking she'd done the day before, and she'd slept fitfully, awakening often preoccupied with images of the dead bodies and the very much living, very fine body of Sadie Barnes. Clashing pictures that aroused different parts of Mary's body.

She wondered why someone from Big Bottom Foods was in town and how he ended up dead. She puzzled over Win having lifted a wallet and considered he might have more booty hidden in multiple places. She glared at him. Certainly, he didn't have the strength to carry off a gun. Still she would need to find his every cache and inventory the bird's plunder. The thought of chasing after him exhausted her further. Like Sadie had said, "neither of them was getting any younger."

Maybe it was these thoughts that caused her to do the impulsive thing she did next.

When the same high school kid—Jimmy Royce—came into Mary's store, she looked at him and decided she liked him. "You working the Carnival?"

"I hope so. I signed up yesterday. Mom said she didn't want any of us under her feet any more for the rest of summer. She doesn't care whether we find paid work, volunteer, or run away. She just wants us all gone. She said something about the French Foreign Legion."

Mary laughed. She supposed all parents felt that way one time or another. Had she been so often under her own mother's feet that her mother left rather than ask her to find a job?

Jimmy took a can of Coke from the cooler, placed a dollar on the counter, opened the can and took a long swig.

Mary stared at the boy and said a silent prayer. "Are you honest?"

He hesitated but said, "Yeah."

"Would you take a paid job?" *Great God, what am I saying? I'll be broke before the week's out.*

This question elicited more energy.

"Yeah! You got one for me? What is it?"

"Working here in the store."

"Oh, yeah, of course. Dumb question." He reddened up and bobbed around on his feet.

Mary knew the polite thing to say was that there weren't any dumb questions, but in her experience, there were lots of dumb questions in the world and she swore she'd been asked many of them repeatedly.

"Check with your folks. If they're all right with you taking a job here, you can start training tomorrow."

"If I call my mom now and she gives permission, may I start now?"

Mary grew a little suspicious, but she grinned. "I like you. Call her up. I need you competent enough to cover me when I'm working my shifts at the Carnival."

"What about the serial killer? Will there even be a Carnival?"

"There'll be a Carnival." The strength in her own voice made Mary feel like a woman in charge. "For summer I want you a couple hours every day during the week, longer if I have any money left, there's need, and you're available. Once school starts, I need you two hours after school during the week, and depending on how you do, there may be some weekend hours, especially early morning on Saturday. It pays minimum wage, $7.75 an hour." Mary wished she could get away with paying less, but she obeyed the law.

"Plus, I'll feed you if you abide leftovers or chips, pop, and sandwiches from the store. No having friends loitering about the store, no stealing or eating away my profits. Be prompt, courteous, and friendly. Count the change carefully—leave the big bills on top of the drawer while you make change. When the store's not busy, it's your job to restock the shelves and assemble things like charcoal grills and display items. You think you can handle those things?"

"I've never assembled a grill or displayed anything."

"You'll learn. There are instructions. Besides, I heard that a person can learn to do almost anything by watching a YouTube video."

"Bullshit," Win squawked.

"I've been watching YouTube episodes on building a roof garden," she added.

"What about if I have a band concert or get into a play or one of the sports teams gets dangerously low on players and asks me to join?" Jimmy asked Mary the question but stared at Win.

"You're off. Heck, I may close the store to watch you. I love watching school activities. I used to go to about every concert, play, and game with my father. It's important to see high school students doing something other than being smartasses."

He bought a Snickers candy bar and called his mom on his cell phone.

Mary'd shocked herself. She'd never hired any helpers, not even during Carnival, as Sadie had been quick to remind her the day prior. Now she'd hired a helper. An observant person might conclude that Mary was heedlessly throwing her money around or trying to free up her time. No, she wasn't ready to admit that to anyone or herself, nor was she about to let herself think of how she might use that extra time. She was already judging herself for spending the extra money.

Jimmy smiled and put two dollars on the counter for the notebook he'd found in a rack nearby. Then he put his phone in his pocket and saluted Mary. "Jimmy Royce reporting for duty, Ms. Caine. Mom said to give you her thanks and to tell you a more formal thank-you will follow."

"Your mom actually thanked me for hiring you?"

"I told you she wants us out of the house. You know, Ms. Caine."

"You can call me Mary."

"You know, Mary. I have good grades—some of the best— but my mom doesn't want me in the house even if I'm reading."

"Well, you can be here and if your work is done, you can read."

"Do you have Internet?" he asked.

"Nope, my store is a dead zone."

"Really? I didn't think there were any more signal dead zones in town."

"Oh, the signal makes it here all right. It's just that I will only pay for Internet over my dead body. Hence, dead zone."

Jimmy stood in front of the chalkboard.

"You can write poetry and math equations on that wall of blackboard if you want. In fact, I would love it if you would sketch the outline of Africa on the board. Chalk in the borders of countries as best you can. Consider it running a special—a free candy bar for each country correctly labeled on the map, one per person of course."

Jimmy smiled. "I'll look on my phone and do the outline today. Why Africa?"

"I don't know. St. Cloud folks have had their undies in a bunch over immigrants from Somalia. I thought it would be good to show a map of where Somalia is located. You know it's along the coast of the Indian Ocean? I bet it is beautiful, but no place is beautiful if you and your family are surrounded by civil war. I'll tape up another map with the names of the countries filled in."

"Why would you give the answers too?"

"The point isn't making people feel stupid about not knowing every country in Africa. The point is getting people interested in new information."

He nodded. "I bought this notebook to write down the important things you tell me. I want to do a good job."

Maybe he was worth the extra expense. She liked him even more. "Another thing—let me know anything you hear about those dead bodies or the Carnival. You need to be my eyes and ears on the ground, Jimmy. Win will cover the skies." She pointed to the cage.

"Yes, Mary."

Mary slid a key across the counter to the boy. It had been her key since her father first gave it to her. She'd use his from now on.

"The first thing you do when you get here is turn all the lights on, put the money from the bank deposit bag in the drawer of the cash register, and prepare a quote of the day."

"Man, I don't know that I can think of something smart to say every single day." Jimmy scratched his head.

"Lucky for both of us that this part of the store ethos is not dependent on you or me alone." Mary pointed to a small stack of notebooks behind the counter. "My dad wrote down quotes from a number of amazing minds—Carl Rogers, Roy Rogers, and Fred Rogers; the Dali Lama to Dolly Parton; Saint Paul, Saint John, George and Ringo and William H. Gass. No lack of irony there.

"Some of the quotes are about God, some are about fishing, life, and death, and some are about baseball. Pick something from the notebook and write it on the wall. Make certain you cite the source. It's done for today, but maybe you could pick something for tomorrow. You can still write it up there with tomorrow's date."

He thumbed through the top notebook—a small moleskin journal with broken spine. "It must be very special to have notebooks written by your father especially since he's…"

"Dead?"

"Yeah."

"It is. I think sometimes he wrote down beautiful quotes to make amends for things he wished he'd never said. He said 'Jesus Christ' a lot even though he wasn't praying." Mary picked up one of the notebooks. "It makes me feel close to him knowing what he thought was important enough to add to a notebook. I see his handwriting and it's like there's this trail of connection between us through my memories. The people we have loved are never totally gone."

"What about that man by the lake? Nobody knows who he is to tell the family what happened to him."

"The sheriff knows now, thanks to Win. Long story, but even if he didn't there's somebody who senses his absence. He'll be known and remembered." Mary finished stocking the gum and breath mints.

"What do you think?" Jimmy pointed at the wall that Mary had painted to make a giant chalkboard. He had written: "The life of the dead is placed in the memories of the living."—Cicero.

"Well done, Jimmy."

As she watched him throughout the day she grew more and more fond of the boy. Had she brought this much joy and fascination to her father as he watched her learn the job? She noted when his two hours were up and calculated his wage, but she didn't tell him to leave. She asked him to work longer.

She liked the way he hung on her every instruction and took notes. Mary had never experienced that before. She wondered if parenting felt like that sometimes before kids begin to hate their parents.

Jimmy was courteous, his math was passable, and he bagged items with a mind that had some awareness of geometry and physical science—or maybe the side benefits of video games. Mostly, Mary liked the way he smiled and had the thoughtfulness to ask people if they needed help getting their groceries to their cars. He was a young man who could think outside himself. Mary considered offering the Royce family a discount for their exceptional parenting. She flicked that idea out of her head. After all, she was saving to put in a roof garden.

CHAPTER EIGHT

The Girl

Relief washed over Mary, noticing Jimmy wanted to wait on most of the young people who happened into the store. It wasn't that she didn't like kids and teens. She liked them a lot, but she didn't know how to talk to them without sounding like she was advising them of some great truth or yelling at them or both.

A few of the boys leaned across the counter to share a joke or something with Jimmy. Mary was impressed with Jimmy and with herself for having spotted him and hired him. Her admiration dissipated late in the afternoon on Jimmy's second day, however. Becoming distracted, he dropped an open roll of pennies and crushed bananas beneath canned tomatoes while he bagged, and he'd given out the wrong change several times.

Finally Mary asked him, "What's with you? It's like you have forgotten everything you learned."

"Nothing. I'm fine. It's just her." He pointed out the front window like a bird dog recognizing prey. Across the street a young girl sat on the bench in front of the bank.

"Who is she? I don't have my binoculars." Mary swayed back and forth peering out the front glass window. She speculated that it was the Hanley kid but couldn't be certain.

"That's Sarah Hanley."

Mary walked back, leaned over, rested her elbows on the counter and her chin on her hands looking up at Jimmy, and teased, "What's your interest? She your girlfriend?"

"No way. I didn't have nothing to do with…her."

Mary stood up again like a mature primate. "What're you so jumpy about? She's a pretty girl, smart. I see her name on the honor roll along with yours. Look, she's reading a book or something. She's got a lot of things going for her and many of those things she has in common with you."

"Yeah, she's wicked smart. I'm not talking about that. Kids say she's you know."

Oh God, what was he stammering about? Mary expected he was going to say the girl was a suspected Democrat, but he surprised her.

He leaned in, "She's pg, pregnant." His face reddened like a blister, and his brow furrowed as he looked at Mary. Perhaps he was expecting shock and awe.

"Hmm. Do you think it was the Holy Spirit?"

"What? No." He turned to Mary.

"Then why're you so flustered? There was somebody else involved, she's not alone in this. It was probably some boy in her class."

Silence.

"Wait, she's in your class."

Jimmy nodded in the affirmative.

"Have you impregnated a high school girl?" Mary reached back and grabbed a box of condoms, paying no attention to the fact that she had chosen a brand advertised to be extra-large, ribbed, and strawberry-flavored. She placed the condoms on the counter. "There you go, a present from me." She felt a slight twinge. Condoms weren't as cheap as they should be. She added, "Don't mention it to your mom unless you know she'd approve."

He picked up the box of condoms like they might burn his hands and placed them back on the shelf. "I didn't impregnate anybody, and my mom would kill me if I did—actually she said she'd castrate me with a rusty scissors first and then she'd kill me."

"Ooh, harsh." Mary raised a howdy wave to some new customers, but she stared at Sarah Hanley. She forgot about Jimmy's discomfort. She felt for the girl. She could only imagine what it would be like being pregnant and facing her last year of high school. A smart girl with diminishing options. The thought of it pained Mary. After a minute or so, Mary slapped her knee. "That's it." Mary rounded the counter on her way out of the store.

"Do you think you can concentrate on your work long enough for me to take a walk? I have no expectations of you bringing in great profits but try not to damage too many things. I'd like to at least break even today. Come on, Bob."

"Gravid," Win said and then whistled.

"Okay, you can go too, but be back before closing."

Win left his cage grumbling something Mary couldn't understand.

Mary left the store, crossed the street, and slowly approached Sarah Hanley. The girl's eyes were red and glassy like she'd been crying. Mary supposed there was a lot of that for a girl in her position. Sarah held a specimen bottle up and examined the blackish, leggy thing inside it.

"What have you got there?" Mary sat on the bench next to the girl.

"Mayor Carl found this giant water bug. He gave it to my mom for my collection. I came into town to get a kill jar and rubbing alcohol from the science lab." She continued staring at the insect from all sides. "Look, they wear their bones on the outside. I can keep it just like this for years and it will look just like the creature I recognize today."

"Beautiful in its own way, I guess."

"I think so. People die and the things we recognize about them, skin, hair, muscle, water, and fats rot away from secret bones." She wiped her eyes and lowered the terminal bug.

Bob Barker rested his head on Sarah's leg. She scratched him behind his ears.

"I'm Mary Caine."

"I know. Everybody knows who you are…because of your store and…" The girl stopped talking.

"What? Because I'm still gay or was a big drunk?" Mary surprised herself by being so blunt. She also thought it was a sad situation if Sarah held Mary's alcoholism against her. After all, Mary was now sober. The same couldn't be said for Sarah's mom, Karen, if gossip was to be believed. Mary poked herself inside for having that thought and flashed a prayer and amends east of town to the Hanley place.

"Is it true that you hired Jimmy Royce to work at your store?"

"How did you find that out so quickly? He just started yesterday."

"His mom called my mom. Mom said you never hire any help. Are you dying?"

"Not that I know of, but none of us are promised tomorrow."

"I guess you're right."

"Funny that you mention that—hiring Jimmy, I mean—not me dying. I was wondering if you're looking for a job. I just hired Jimmy and he's doing a bang-up job. I was thinking that if one senior is good for my store maybe two would be better. I could use some more help this whole summer and during the Carnival, of course. I'd want you after school and weekends during the school year. You interested in working in my store?"

"Interested? I'd start this minute, but I promised my mom I'd have her car back. Can I call my mom and see if she'll let me be in town a while longer? Could I start today?"

What was it with these teens? Hadn't they heard they were supposed to be lazy, shiftless morons and resentful of entry-level employment? Or was this all a masterfully orchestrated conspiracy to rid Mary of her money?

"Yes, that'd be great. The sooner you start the sooner you learn the job and become useful."

"What do you pay?"

"Minimum wage."

"Could I earn more than that if I work hard?"

"You get minimum wage for working hard. You earn more than minimum wage for showing initiative." Mary liked the girl's spunk.

Sarah tilted her head, put her specimen bottle on the bench, stood up and put out her hand. "May I study at work if my duties are completed and there's no one needing my help?"

"I would expect nothing less."

"I'll take the job, but I'm going to need as many hours as you can possibly give me."

Mary's stomach clutched.

"In case you haven't heard, my baby is due in December. My mom said she'll watch it until I graduate in spring and then I need to be on my own like she was when she had me. That's how it works."

So that's how it works. Good to know.

She placed her free hand on her belly. "I have some money, but I'll need a lot more to live on my own." She put her free hand into the pocket of her jeans.

Mary nodded. "Welcome to the staff of Caine's General Store. I'm the general. You call your mom. I hope to see you at the store in a few minutes. I could use your help every day of the week if you're free."

What in the hell am I doing? Do I want to be poor and alone instead of just alone?

Bob Barker barked and wagged his tail.

"Can I just say one more thing, Ms. Caine?"

"You may if you call me Mary."

"Well, Mary, I want you to know that I'm not staying in this town, baby or no baby. I'm going to college. There wasn't much here for me before and there's nothing now." She touched her belly again. "The Dollars for Scholars' group is giving away two $20,000 scholarships from the money they get from the service clubs who run the Carnival. I'm going to win one of those and go to college and study biology or possibly entomology. Do you know what that is?"

"I do, and it doesn't bug me at all."

They both smiled.

Sarah dug her cell phone from her pocket and began to press the buttons.

"Come on, Bob. Back to work." Mary returned to the store. Inside Jimmy Royce was fidgeting like an untrained puppy. She was relieved he hadn't yet piddled on the floor.

"What did you say to her? Did you tell what I told you? I hope you didn't. She'll never talk to me."

Mary knew the next words out of her mouth would either tranquilize him or possibly cause him to spontaneously combust. Both options seemed like interesting viewing. "I hired her." Jimmy quieted right down but then cowered like a whipped dog.

"Am I fired?"

"Hell, no. You've been promoted. You are senior staff and in charge of the training of junior staff and part of a workforce of three. She's calling her mom to see if she can start today."

Jimmy looked like he might faint.

"Are you okay with that? I want you to help me train her in at the cash register. She needs this money and a scholarship just like you."

He nodded. "I'll be fine. I'm just surprised."

"I have to take an inventory of the meat. Another thing— bring up one of those barstools with the footrest and padded back. Put it up here at the counter. She may need to sit some if she's carrying a baby."

As Mary counted packages of beef, pork, and chicken, Jimmy retrieved the high stool. He chose the red one over the black one. He removed the price tag and asked Mary how she wanted to address the change in inventory.

"You're learning quickly, Mr. Royce. Place the tag in the notebook I use to record business expenses. Date it. I think the three of us are going to make a formidable team."

Jimmy had little time to panic if he was panicking. Sarah walked into the store only minutes later. The two looked at one another.

"Hey."

"Hey."

"Jimmy's going to show you the ropes, Sarah. He's learned everything very quickly and I suspect you will too." Mary lifted her head, stroked her neck, and allowed herself to sound philosophical. "Working a grocery store is like running a large lemonade stand. There's product, customers, and the counting of money. Smile, be polite, add, and subtract. That's all there is to it. Hell, it can't be too complicated. I've been doing it for years."

CHAPTER NINE

A Boy and a Girl

Over the next couple days Mary's new hires found their sea legs at the store like they were born to it. Mary gave them each a key so they could open the store. They posted the quote of the day, stocked, and waited on customers, and together they had made a reasonable chalk drawing of the continent of Africa on the blackboard. Each day they arrived in the morning for "a few hours of work" and Mary kept them all day. At the end of the day they asked if they should return and Mary pretended to contemplate the question, but said yes, she could use them for "a few hours of work."

Additionally, they absorbed bits of information and relayed it to Mary with speed.

"I heard…" Jimmy began.

"Bullshit," squawked Win.

"I did too!" Jimmy turned to Mary. "Why does that bird do that?"

"Ignore him. What did you hear?"

"I heard that the sheriff ran the plates on a car parked by the lake. The car belongs to someone from Bloomington."

"Bloomington. Interesting. I'm going to stock the cereal." Mary already knew this.

Jimmy gained some ease around Sarah, and Sarah's confidence and hard-earned exoskeleton didn't seem to thwart him. He seemed to occasionally fixate on Sarah's belly, but Mary guessed it was better than always staring at Sarah's breasts like some boys might.

Sarah could handle herself.

"You want to touch my stomach or something? You keep staring at it like an alien might pop out and splash blood all over."

"I wasn't... Yeah, I was. I'm sorry. I just keep thinking about there being a baby in there." Jimmy lowered his head and squinted.

"It's kind of freaky." Sarah put her hand on her abdomen. "There's another person growing inside me. Sometimes I think about the cells dividing and becoming tissue and organs and I am blown away at the complexity. By now the baby is only five centimeters head to rump but fully formed. That's less than two inches." Sarah spread her thumb and forefinger to illustrate her point. "He or she has ears, toes, fingers with fingernails, and it has the genitals that determine its gender."

"Elephants are pregnant for twenty-two months." Jimmy continued to stare at her belly.

"Well, I'm glad I'm not carrying an elephant. God, Jimmy."

"You'd need a bigger stool."

Sarah laughed and then she turned to Jimmy, her face deathly serious. "Sometimes, I just think about how much the baby will need from me and I want to pretend it's not there." Sarah sighted Jimmy in, pointed at him, and spoke more sternly. "Don't tell anybody that I told you that. I'll deny it."

"I won't say anything to anyone. It makes sense. You know, I have seven little brothers and sisters and two older sisters."

"So? What are you saying?" Sarah had a hand on her hips.

As Mary eavesdropped she wasn't certain what Jimmy was getting at either.

"I'm just saying I know something about having kids, even babies around. Sometimes, I wish I could pretend they aren't there, but most days I'm glad to be part of a big family. Maybe I could be a help to you." He looked at Sarah like she might be Santa Claus and then lowered his head like he suspected he was on the naughty list. "I'm sorry." Jimmy looked down with his head swaying like a listless baby elephant. "I'm sorry. You probably have a million friends you like better than me to help."

Sarah laughed. "Is that what you think?"

"What? You think I'm lame, don't you? Just forget about it." Jimmy looked like he'd been slapped. He hoisted a case of snack-size bags of potato chips and cheese snacks onto the counter, sliced the tape with his box cutter, and began stocking the shelves near the register and the metal grid.

"Jimmy, I'm not saying you're lame. It's just that my so-called 'girlfriends' haven't said anything about wanting to help. They've just talked shit about me behind my back. Boys stay away from me like I might explode or accuse them of being the father." She quickly wiped a tear away from her eye and glanced at Jimmy. "I suppose they think I'm a slut and a pretty stupid slut at that." Her words hung in the air as more of a question than a statement.

Mary wanted to break in here, soothe the girl, but then she would have to give up her position by the dry cereal and admit she had been eavesdropping all along. Before Mary could will her legs out of the squatting position that allowed her to place the most sugary cereals on the bottom shelf, Jimmy spoke up to Sarah.

"I don't think you're a slut. I've never said that or even thought that."

Tears came to Mary's eyes. She sat down on her bottom so that she could continue to hear and see her stellar employees without being seen herself or interrupting their talk.

Jimmy swallowed and watched Sarah. He hadn't hit the growth spurt that would show what he'd look like as a man. His brown hair was still thin and poorly cut. He wasn't particularly muscled, but he was handsome with dark eyes and an easy smile. More than that, Mary felt like he had a good core. Which makes even plain or ugly attractive.

Sarah smiled shyly but didn't speak. She didn't have an ounce of extra fat stretching her perfect skin. Her pregnancy thickened her middle a bit, but otherwise she was thin with small breasts. Her auburn hair barely reached her shoulders.

Jimmy continued, "I don't think that the father of your baby is a stud or any of the other stupid names people come up with for people who do things that anybody could've done—not that you would have had sex with just anybody." He had finished stocking the chips. He broke down the box as he talked. "Guys, most guys, are always talking about wanting to have sex or bragging that they have already."

Sarah rolled her eyes and laughed.

"It's true. You should hear them. Actually, no, you shouldn't hear us. We're disgusting. My mom says starting at age twelve all boys should be put in military school not because she wants us to be soldiers, but because then the rest of civilized society wouldn't have to listen to us or smell us."

Sarah laughed. "Thinking about the other boys in our class, I can see why your mom said that. The guy, you know…"

"The father?"

"Yeah, he was sweet and maybe he meant all the things he said when he said them. He gave me… I don't even know if I can keep it." She shook her head. A tear fell on her cheek that she quickly wiped away. "It doesn't matter now." She spritzed the counter with a cleaner and wiped it with a paper towel. "I don't even care. It's not like I was in love with him and wanted to get married or anything. It's impossible now." Sarah sat on the stool and swiveled.

"Don't you ever want to get married?" Jimmy moved on to stocking Snickers, Reese's Peanut Butter Cups, and Kit Kat bars.

"Maybe I'll want to get married if I meet someone I love, and he…" Sarah stood up. She straightened the gum and mints. "For right now, I need to study so I can get a scholarship, work here, have my baby, and then figure out a way to go to college. Falling in love and marriage are way down my list of priorities."

Jimmy nodded his head. "I hope the Carnival isn't canceled."

"Don't even say it. If the Carnival doesn't happen, I won't get that scholarship and I'm stuck here. Where will I live? I can't live with my mom. Even if she would let me, I wouldn't want to."

Jimmy didn't say it, but Mary knew he was hoping for a scholarship too.

Sarah approached the drawing of Africa on the chalkboard and put Tunisia on the apostrophe-shaped country in northeastern Africa. Jimmy stood beside her. She handed him the chalk and he marked in Chad.

The bell on the front door rang as a few customers filtered in. Jimmy and Sarah returned to the counter, both smiling and attentive. Mary finished stocking the sweet cereal but filed the even sweeter conversation into her memory folder of moments of grace. She thought, but only fleetingly, about the money it was costing to have staff. The young people's competence gave Mary the leisure to devote only cursory attention to her own store responsibilities. This freedom of thought left more room for her preoccupation with the Carnival and Sadie Barnes.

CHAPTER TEN

The Gossip

Later that evening, the front of Mary's store filled spontaneously. Jimmy left for home after his shift, but Sarah had asked to work some extra hours straightening and light stocking. Mary was glad Sarah had asked to stay although she didn't like paying for extra hours. A few people looked at the chalkboard for the specials. Somebody marked Egypt, South Africa, and Morocco on the map of Africa but didn't request a complimentary candy bar.

From what she could gather the sudden onslaught was related to an emergency meeting of the Lions Club executive committee, which had expanded to include the Women's Club executive committee and suddenly the full membership. Although the meeting had taken place over the dinner hour, they had not eaten, nor had they successfully finished everything on their meeting agenda. Mary's neighbors were unsettled.

Mary was glad Sarah was still at work and could manage the register while she bagged and listened. She flashed a prayer as she watched and caught pieces of conversation. Routine carnival business was mixed with gesticulations of worry and foreboding. Gessell, Mielke, and Loven perused a paper with the band bookings. Mary pictured the crowds pressing the pavilion band shell. She had never had the comfort in her body to dance on the dance floor but envied those who danced with abandon. When she was a kid that dance floor had been a tennis court. Her body hadn't been much more comfortable with a tennis racket.

Beseman and Oven showed Mary the raffle ticket sales projections. She bought two of the hundred-dollar tickets, which was the precedent her father had begrudgingly established. The big raffle drawing was held on Sunday afternoon. First prize was five thousand dollars, but smaller cash prizes amounted to several thousand more.

At a certain point the conversations grew louder and more animated. Olson almost gestured as he talked with Nelson.

Sarah dropped a roll of dimes.

Golombecki said, "We just accepted the bid on five thousand dollars' worth of chicken. What the hell will we do with all that chicken if we can't cook it and sell it at Carnival?"

"What do you mean?" Mary asked. "There won't be *chicken* at the Carnival?" She began to hyperventilate.

No one said anything, but the mood was pensive.

She had seen the operation involved in readying that chicken for the Carnival. Case upon case of four-pound whole chickens arrived for preparation and storage. Women and men used band saws to quarter all the whole chickens and cut them into eight pieces, putting some of the chicken aside for pan-frying. The chicken was sorted and tubbed. The tubs of chicken were dumped into a sausage mixer where the chicken was seasoned. Forty-five hundred servings of chicken would be sold over the three-day Carnival, most of it slathered in that signature barbeque sauce.

Gessell talked into her cell phone as she marked a half dozen African countries on the map. Mary assumed Pfeffer, the club's lawyer, was on the other side of the call. "You better get over to the courthouse, Pfeff, and stop that injunction." She nodded at Mary.

Mary asked after each one's family and performed the death math with each of them who she knew had lost parents or siblings in recent years. Some talked to Win. Somebody asked when she was going to finally roast the oversized parrot.

Mary strained her ears to take in all the surrounding conversations as she bagged groceries. She learned there was a squadron of Big Bottom Foods executives and their corporate attorneys in town claiming their company had successfully purchased the preliminary rights to market and produce the Midsummer Carnival Barbeque Sauce and their rights precluded Whistler's use of said recipe for the upcoming carnival. The profit on chicken alone ran between fifteen and twenty thousand. No chicken for sale would take a big bite out of the bottom line.

"Kavanaugh." Someone who sounded like Mayor Carl said the name like he might spit afterward. "McConnell Kavanaugh was the Big Bottom guy dead on the shore."

That was the first time Mary had heard the dead guy's complete name from anyone other than the sheriff. She assumed that the name being out in public meant his identity had been confirmed and his people notified. They would have their own death math same as the Latiskee family.

"I'd like to find the man Kavanaugh talked to and wring his neck." Swisher folded his six-foot five frame as he dug a Drumstick ice cream treat out of Mary's ice cream freezer. "Who would be that stupid to think they could get away with selling that recipe?"

"What would that matter? I thought most everybody on the Carnival planning committee knew that recipe." Mary restocked some single cans of soda.

A hush fell over the grocery store like Mary had accidently said, "fuck."

"What?" Mary looked at each shocked face in turn.

"Yeah, you're right, Mary. It's not that we need that recipe to make the sauce, but if we no longer own the recipe, we can't make it. There's an official, certified copy owned by the town, but it's missing." Johnson leaned in closer to Mary at the counter. "Big Ass Foods is saying that Kavanaugh fellow brokered a deal with…" he hesitated a moment… "a teacher and that he came to town to pay for the certified copy and that he got it the night he died by the lake."

"A teacher?" Coach Natvig said. "That's bullshit!"

Berge and Thompson took cold drinks from the cooler. Berge said, "There's a court hearing today. Big Bottom Foods is saying they now own the recipe and we can't use it for Carnival without their permission or giving them a share in the profits—they're asking sixty percent."

"What happened to the certified copy of the recipe?" Mary asked.

"Nobody knows," Van Norman said.

"What happened to the money is a better question," Primus said.

Johnson explained. "Big Bottom Foods is saying that someone from Whistler had already accepted a cashier's check for five thousand dollars in exchange for a copy of that recipe with the understanding that after BB Foods replicated it in their test kitchen and approved of it, they'd buy it."

Sarah dropped a roll of nickels.

"That's horseshit." Coach Natvig stepped forward. "How can they replicate that recipe?"

Mary knew that the football coach knew his shit. She'd never been privy to that part of the Carnival preparation but making that barbeque sauce recipe was a thing of lore. The task had to be learned by mentorship. It was a position of honor and responsibility.

A week before the Carnival a team made about one hundred and seventy-five gallons of the tangy sauce. It was said the sauce was cooked in a modified duck boat over a wood-burning stove stoked with cedar logs. That was a lie, of course. It was cooked in a modified duck boat on a gas stove at the school cafeteria kitchen.

The boat wasn't new and wasn't exactly level. Crevices where the seats had been removed posed a particular challenge during cooking. The person tending the sauce had to stir carefully and continuously in some areas so the sauce didn't burn. They stirred it with an aluminum canoe paddle.

"Anyway," Johnson continued, "if the sauce passed muster with their focus groups, which apparently it did, Big Bottom would pay another twenty thousand dollars when Kavanaugh took possession of the certified copy. Sheriff says neither check was on Kavanaugh and we don't know who he paid the deposit to prior to his meeting and death."

Mary preferred to work with smaller wholesalers, but she could easily picture Big Bottom acquiring a product like Whistler's Carnival barbeque recipe, substituting whatever it could with corn syrup, mass producing it, and distributing it to independent grocery outlets across the Midwest.

"Big Butt must know who they wrote a check to."

"They probably do, but they aren't saying. They're saying it was a cashier's check and that Kavanaugh was the only person who knew the identity of the local source or sources." Peterson put a few groceries on the counter for Mary to tally and bag.

Mary handed Peterson his change. "What does this have to do with Buddy?"

"Don't know. Maybe nothing." Nelson put a package of hot dog buns on the counter next to some old-fashioned wieners. "Buddy was a newish member of the Lions Club, but he hadn't attended many meetings. He did some carpentry work for us at the park building a while back."

"I thought when those companies bought a recipe they paid money for the recipe and then royalties from sales on top." Mary bagged Nelson's groceries.

"It's something like that," Johnson said. "I guess the terms depend on whoever is brokering the deal. Right now, we don't know for certain who did it, but whoever did it didn't have the approval of our clubs."

A voice came from the canned food aisle. "We know who did it. There were witnesses."

A chorus of "shut up" and "shut your pie hole" followed.

Mary looked at her neighbors' faces. *What aren't you telling me?*

"Help yourself to a free soda if you'd like." Mary nodded at the cooler.

And suddenly everybody is thirsty.

"Well, you're sure throwing your money around, Mary Caine. I heard you were thinking of making a roof garden too. Maybe you got the money from Big Bottom Foods." Coach Natvig laughed as he said it, but Mary knew that the whole thing was stirring up suspicion between neighbors and friends. There wasn't a soul in Whistler who couldn't use a boost of five thousand dollars.

"Not me. I haven't sold anything and certainly wouldn't sell something that wasn't mine to sell. You said witnesses. What did they see?"

"You know, Mary, we miss you at the beer garden," Coach Natvig said.

His words hung in the air like he might have lit a fuse.

Oh, the beer garden where a person could buy beer from any of the four sides of the spacious booth. In recent years like the food booths and rides people bought tickets to pay for their beer. Mary easily pictured the translucent, sixteen-ounce plastic cups filled with the amber succor and she knew she mustn't dwell on the image very long.

She diffused the tension with a laugh. "I'll be sure to buy extra pie and chicken to make up for my lack of beer consumption. There'll be plenty of people drinking beer who don't have a problem with alcohol like I realized I do." Mary was grateful when Borgert changed the subject back to the barbeque recipe.

Borgert, who always saw the good in people said, "No sane person in Whistler would sell that recipe without guaranteed allowances for using it at the Carnival." He took a can of Coke from the cooler.

"We could jot down a list of the insane people in town or maybe we could spread the word that whoever did it could just return the recipe and the money, apologize to the town, and start over? Problem solved."

All the shoppers froze in place and looked at Mary like she might have suggested letting a daycare class loose to play on the interstate or suggested snake handling as a high school sport.

"What?"

"Great advice from someone who doesn't have any money worries." Mary's stomach burned. She couldn't see who said this, but it wasn't news to her that her family money was a sore spot for some people.

"I don't think anybody's feeling very forgiving toward whoever did this." Tepley slowly shook his head.

The sound of a glass jar hitting the floor in Aisle Three turned heads. "Mary, I owe you for a jar of pickles," Mayor Carl said.

The bell above the door rang as someone left the store. Mary didn't see who it was.

"Already volunteers are canceling," Nelson said. "I guess the thinking is, why should people volunteer if somebody took all that money and didn't put it into the town? Some people think it had to be someone from the Lions' or Women's Club because they had to have access to the certified copy kept in a locked cabinet in the office at the park building."

"No signs of any break-in?" Mary asked Johnson.

"Nope." Johnson took a swig of his pop.

"Who has the key?"

Johnson and a half dozen other men fished key rings from their pockets and dangled little gold keys in the air like they were bell ringers. "Hell, who doesn't have a key?"

Mary didn't. "Why bother to lock something if so many people have the key?"

"It was Mayor Carl's idea back in the day when he actually was mayor." Nelson looked around the store. "Where is he? He was here a few minutes ago. It was his idea that the executive board should all have keys so that Carnival business and town improvements could be conducted promptly."

Town improvements was an understatement. Mary and everybody else knew it. Those clubs were Whistler's life support. Thanks to the Lions, Women's Club, and other civic groups Whistler had things like a renovated swimming beach on Little Swan, park buildings and playground equipment, a new fire engine, streetlights, and scholarships for graduating seniors. The Midsummer Carnival was the premium venue for these groups to raise funds. There were local businesses that benefitted from contracts, but the money didn't go into any one person's pocket. The funds were put back into the community. Volunteering was a rite of passage—a bartering that kept traditions alive. High school kids helped with the daily cleanup and bingo to earn money for events like senior prom. Whistler was dependent on those service clubs and their two hundred volunteers to make the Carnival happen.

Borgert added, "It's not like there's any cash in that cabinet and no one thought anybody'd mess with that recipe."

"I guess that there isn't much somebody won't mess with if it gets them some money." Mary leaned against the counter.

"The notion that somebody sold that recipe for personal gain has put people off volunteering or even going to the Carnival. It may be a loss this year." Thieschafer put a small beef roast on the counter next to a bag of yellow onions and some organic carrots.

"The two kids I hired here at the store are good students. I think they're both hoping to win a scholarship from Dollars for Scholars."

People nodded. Many of them had kids or relatives who had or would benefit from scholarship money generated by the service clubs. Each family tried to make the plight of the next generation easier than it was for them. The despair of what they didn't know and what might occur sat on the shoulders of Mary's friends and neighbors. They stooped under the weight of the unknown and suspicions that were poisoning the community as effectively as a tainted water supply.

Quietly, slowly, the store cleared out. Sarah lingered.

"You can go, Sarah. I can finish the rest of the closing." Mary began spritzing down the counter. "Is your mom coming to get you?"

"I'll call her in a minute. Can I ask you a question?"

"Of course."

"If a person did something bad, but then also did something good, would that make the bad not as bad?"

"If you're talking black market organ procurement, it's still bad, especially if they have their eyes on my organs. Besides, the doctor told me my liver wasn't even good enough to serve with onions."

"Okay. I'm sorry. It was a dumb question."

"No, I'm sorry I made a joke. It's a good and complex question that philosophers, ethicists, and theologians have battled for centuries. For me it comes down to my faith and my program, which coincides quite a bit. If I do wrong and do something right with the bounty of my wrong, then I have to make amends or ask for forgiveness.

"What I'm saying is that there is always a way back to God or other people if we admit our wrongs and try to correct them and do better. Nobody has to hold their mistakes—everybody makes them—until they fester and poison their lives. Does that make sense?"

"I think so. I'll wait outside while I call my mom. See you tomorrow." Sarah left the store. Mary locked the door behind her.

Mary was left to her own thoughts. What was Sarah's ethical dilemma? More pressing, what about these witnesses? Thinking about witnesses brought her back to thinking about Win. Somehow, he had ended up with Kavanaugh's wallet. Why was the wallet wet? Mary looked up at the bird perched in his cage. What if the bird had more evidence?

"What do you know about all this, Win?" Win was silent, but Mary suspected he was watching for the next opportunity to fly out the door.

CHAPTER ELEVEN

Recon

The next day when Jimmy and Sarah arrived for work Mary asked them to watch the store while she retrieved something upstairs. When she returned, she placed two sets of binoculars on the counter and two fifty-dollar bills.

"I have some extra work for you. In a minute I'm going to shoo that bird out of the store. I will pay you your regular wage plus an extra fifty dollars each if you will watch Win and find his other hiding spots. Use the binoculars and write down for me anytime you see him perch and linger or fiddle around some place in town."

Sarah looked through the binoculars. Then she picked up one of the fifty-dollar bills. "Cool, are you rich?"

"Rich is relative. It just so happens that I had some relatives who amassed some money, so I have a few dollars from a family inheritance from my great-grandmother having invented medical cheese."

"Medical cheese?" Jimmy grimaced.

"It's cringe-worthy, I agree, and dumb, right? Well, she wasn't as dumb as the greedy pharmaceutical rep who bought the patent from her. Great-Grandma invested that money in Standard Oil and IBM. Down the line, my dad converted those stocks into shares of Microsoft and Apple, but I like to say our family made our money from medical cheese."

The two looked at Mary quizzically. "Why are you paying us to follow your bird?" Sarah asked.

"Let's just say I think Win may be a valuable witness to what happened at the lake that night."

"Maybe he's got the money." Jimmy hung the binoculars around his neck. "I heard that somebody in town took a hundred thousand dollars for the barbeque recipe."

"Bullshit," squawked Win.

Sarah bumped the smaller chips display. Mary caught it before it tumbled to the floor.

"Win is right. It was no more than twenty-five thousand involved, maybe only five, and we don't know the whole story yet. There may be some reasonable explanation about what happened."

"Like what?" Jimmy asked.

Mary frowned. "I honestly don't know, but we should all keep an open mind."

"My mom said it was just greed by somebody in one of the service clubs. She said she's not volunteering at the beer garden this year." Sarah placed the fifty-dollar bill back on the counter.

"Sarah, I really don't believe anyone from the service clubs would steal from the town. Getting to the bottom of this makes finding out what happened at the lake necessary and immediate. Our town is being split apart. No amount of money is worth that damage."

"So no one knows what happened to the money?" Sarah asked.

"Somebody knows. God knows. Secrets are hard to keep especially in small towns where people generally have good hearts," Mary said.

"Do you really think Win could help solve what happened at the lake?" Jimmy asked.

"Maybe. He dropped the dead man's wallet on the sheriff's head. Maybe he has some other clues. Why don't you two see if you can spot him and let me know where he hides things."

"Mary, I'd like to go to the Latiskee service. It's tomorrow at eleven in the morning."

"I hadn't heard that," Mary said. "Which church?"

Sarah averted her eyes and then looked back at Mary. "No church. It's at the family farm."

Mary's stomach clenched. "Really?" She reconsidered her plan to attend.

"Yeah, it's a small service," Sarah said. "I'm not telling my mom I'm going."

"Oh. Do you need a ride or someone to go with you?" Mary asked.

"No, I can drive there and then I'll report for work. It shouldn't take too long—the burial is at the cemetery on the edge of their place."

Whistler had a cemetery for the Catholics, another one for the Lutherans, and a small one by the Latiskee farm for the remainders.

"Thanks for telling me. I may close the store during the funeral and burial. I should go too." She wanted to ask Sarah how she became acquainted with Buddy but thought it might sound like she was asking Sarah to justify her desire to be part of this important community ritual.

Mary opened the store door and looked over at Win. "Get out of here, you secretive corvid. Be gone. I know you want to."

Win flew out of his cage and out the door. Sarah and Jimmy ran out after him, pointing at him as he split the sky and swooped away into some trees.

CHAPTER TWELVE

The Losses and Opportunities

Alone in the store Mary sighed and gathered herself before the next wave of customers. Her stomach churned thinking about a funeral for such a young man. She remembered the Koenig boy, the Barber boy, the Swisher girl, the young Pfeffer and Kruzel boys, the Canfield boy, Brenner, and closest to her heart the Thieschafer boy—all young and dying too soon.

She flashed again to the Latiskees' display of grief at the lake. She felt embarrassed and honored to have witnessed something so intimate and so raw. How does a parent survive such a thing? How does a parent survive such a thing when it appears to have been a murder?

If, as the sheriff had said, the stories about Martin Latiskee shooting at people who trespassed on his property were not true, what would the suspicion be after these events? The man she saw at the lake looked like a wounded animal and wounded animals could give up and die or be dangerous.

She forced her mind away from those thoughts. "Think about the Carnival, Mary." Well, that depressed her. What if there was no Carnival? She thought of her mother. There was nothing to say her mother would return this year, but it seemed important that the event happen for an increased probability. She wished she could talk things through with Sadie. Long ago Sadie had praised Mary's sense of hope.

Sadie. When would Mary run into Sadie again? Days had passed since they spoke at the lake. How could she make that happen? Joey Kay's voice rang in her head from her AA meeting the Saturday before. In small group he had said that sometimes he tries to "push the river."

Mary could relate. Hell, she thought she'd dam up the river if it meant she could see Sadie again soon, but she knew she couldn't do anything but wait for her to come to the store. The idea of her going to seek Sadie out was quickly dismissed from her mind as seeming too much like stalking. She had no reason to be at the high school and not enough spine to just show up at Sadie's place. What would people say? What if Sadie sent her away? Mary knew her heart couldn't take it. There wasn't an organ in her body that could take being left by Sadie again.

"Bob, I wonder what the old apartment looks like? Do you think it's the same?" A shiver ran up her neck and back down both arms.

That was the thing about memories and not just bad ones. It took very little of Mary's imagination to remember that apartment, to smell the cut flowers Sadie kept on the table in the kitchen where she rarely cooked. She could almost feel the coolness of Sadie's battered leather couch. It had come from Sadie's grandfather's study and the spicy smell of pipe smoke had still wafted from its cushions if Mary landed on it too heavily. That memory made her cheeks naturally rouge up. It was on that couch she'd first kissed Sadie Barnes or, rather, Sadie had kissed her.

The kiss happened after Mary had known Sadie for most of a year and seen her every day. There'd been no official talk of dating, but she didn't know what else to call what they were doing. Theirs was a very small club with incessant meetings. She knew for a fact there had been boys and men who asked Sadie out. Sadie didn't go out with them, not even for appearances. Mary spent every weekend and many of the weekday evenings at Sadie's apartment, watching movies or reading books while Sadie graded test papers and English compositions. They laughed and talked endlessly over meals that Mary cooked.

The sexual energies that neither one of them acknowledged were sublimated into Mary's cooking, Sadie's eating, and long conversations. By rights they both should have been talked out and the size of minivans. The day of their first kiss was a Saturday after the store had closed. They'd been arguing. Sadie would have said they were debating, but in most circles it would have rightly been called an argument. Sadie had made the assertion that the best type of romance novels or movies were explicit and got right to the romance in full view of the reader.

"Jesus in a convertible! Admit it, Mary, wouldn't you like to see hot steamy kissing and naked bodies?"

"How can you talk about steamy kisses and naked bodies when you won't allow yourself to even swear properly?"

"I swear just fine. You're changing the subject. What's your argument?"

"I don't argue. It's just my opinion that in books, and movies for that matter, I prefer the subtle buildup to romance, then just a taste and most left for the reader's imagination. I have a fully functional imagination." Mary nodded her head, satisfied with her pronouncement.

Then Sadie kissed her right on the lips. Their teeth bumped against each other; Mary's lip was pinched and bled. Sadie pulled back, looked at Mary, and kissed her again. That time Mary was ready. When their lips met, no injuries—the kiss was deep and long. When Sadie had finished, she stood up, head held high, hands on her hips. "There, now tell me how long you would want to wait for that or if you prefer to use your functional imagination of what romance would be like?"

Mary found Sadie's argument compelling. She put out her arms. "I'm going to need more evidence."

Sadie joined Mary back on that leather couch, made such a strong case for explicit romance that the two skipped closing arguments and adjourned to Sadie's bedroom for the rest of the day. Case closed.

Mary didn't dare stay in those memories too long. Although, her body betrayed her intentions. Her breath quickened. She felt faint from the deprivation of love and touch that been her life since that brief love affair. She shook her head and nearly slapped her own cheek. She needed to stay in the present. If she were to meet Sadie again, it would happen because it was meant to be, not by her trying to make it happen. Mary wondered where Sadie was getting her groceries. At that moment the store's front doorbell clanged. Sadie.

Before Sadie could close the door, Win flew into the store, barely missing Sadie's head. He had a white scrap of paper in his thieving jaws. He passed through the store to the backroom.

"Jesus on a unicorn! Was that Win? Mary, I need a few things and I have an invitation for you. Is that bird going to swoop at my head again?"

"Maybe when he comes back from hiding his booty. Actually, Win wasn't swooping at you. He's just opportunistic. He used the opportunity of you opening that door for him to get home again. Besides, Win might be out solving crime. He had that one fellow's wallet in his cage."

"You're kidding me!"

Edwin returned to the front of the store, flew into his cage, and began preening. As he primped in his cage, he giggled as much as crows ever giggle.

Sarah and Jimmy entered the store, winded and perspiring.

"Kids, don't ask the universe a question unless you're ready for an answer." Mary nodded at Sarah and Jimmy. "Did you find anything?"

Sarah's and Jimmy's hangdog looks told Mary they'd had no luck. "Take a break. Eat some ice cream while I serve this demanding customer."

Sadie smiled at the kids. "Hello."

"That's Sarah Hanley and Jimmy Royce. They're seniors." Mary pointed. She felt cheeky. "I've hired them to help me run the store." She casually leaned against the cash register. Error messages emanated from the blamed machine and spoiled what she'd hoped would be a moment. She pressed void and a half a dozen other keys before the contraption stopped squawking.

"You, Mary Caine, hired help? I don't believe it. Are you sure they aren't here on some community service gig and you're taking advantage of free labor?"

"No, I'm paying them."

"What? An hour a week?"

"No, they work every day if they're free. Sarah and Jimmy are making money for college and Sarah is having a baby. They need as many hours as I can give them to help with their futures." Mary's speech surprised her as much as Sadie.

"Well, good. It's about time you spent some your moldy cash on something worthwhile."

Mary let the moldy cash comment slide. Her cash was not moldy. It was accruing paltry interest in the bank, thank you very much. "What can I get for you, Sadie?"

"Breasts."

Before Mary could dispute the assertion, Sadie clarified that she meant chicken breasts.

The mention of chicken breasts deflated Mary. "There might not be barbequed chicken at the Carnival this year. Somebody stole the recipe and tried to sell it to Big Bottom Foods."

"No. That's ridiculous. How could the recipe be stolen?" Sadie looked green.

"Half the town had keys to the cabinet at the park building." Mary pointed to the meat case. "When it comes to fowl, I have several options: chicken breasts, turkey breasts, and lobed tofu and tempeh filets I like to call 'falsies.'"

"Skinless, boneless, chicken breasts from actual chickens will suffice."

Another potential moment lost. "So you cook now?" Mary walked back to the meat cooler and chose a package of chicken breasts.

"I've learned to make a few things; marriage will do that for you." Sadie immediately corrected herself. "Marriage will do that for a person."

"What? Make you learn to cook a few things?"

"Yeah, and other things." Sadie swayed from one foot to the other, perhaps wondering if she had put her foot in her mouth bringing up marriage to her jilted former lover.

"Maybe some time you can tell me about the things your marriage taught you." Mary put her hands on her hips and looked back at Sadie. Then she leaned over the chicken again. "I have breasts—skinless, boneless, antibiotic-free, locally grown, free-range chicken breasts. How many do you need?"

"That depends. Would you come to dinner with me?" Sadie smiled.

Mary grinned. *Praise Higher Power. Would miracles never cease?* "I would love to have dinner with you."

"Great, meet me at six p.m. at Judge Tall's place."

Mary dropped the chicken breasts back in the cooler. "Why would I do that?"

"Because I'm making dinner for you at Judge Tall's house. I assume you know her."

"Everybody without profound hearing loss knows her. She shops here. She likes to quote poetry and berate my produce."

"She suggested I ask you to join us."

"Judge Tall suggested I join you? I suspect that is an untruth, Sadie Barnes. Judge Tall doesn't like me."

"Well, that may be true, but when I consulted her on a legal matter, she suggested you may be able to help me with a certain problem I have."

Mary knew her words came out like a child's whine, but she didn't care. "Why can't we have dinner at your apartment?"

"Judge Tall can't climb those awful steep steps."

"That's good news. She can't sneak up on you."

"I like Judge Tall. She's brilliant and strong. She's sturdy for her age."

"Sturdy? She showed me a picture of herself and her siblings. Hell, they looked like the front line of the eighty-five Chicago Bears except her family has the complexion of white sauce, pasty white." Mary shuddered.

A hot flash of fury and self-pity flushed over her. Sadie had been in town long enough to meet and become a dinner companion with Judge Tall. The jolt must have been hot enough to fry a few brain cells because she went from angry to jealous of the thought of Sadie dining with Judge Tall. "Judge Tall must be at least eighty!"

"So? She still eats." Sadie shook her head as she looked at Mary.

Rightly so. The ridiculousness of Mary's initial reaction smacked her in the head. "Well, of course she does." It felt like a consolation prize. "I'd like to eat with you, and her, any day."

"In that case I will need three chicken breasts—make it four in case her sister is home."

"Good grief, how did this become a dinner party?"

"I need potatoes—the yellow kind you used to cook and greens for a salad, but nothing you think Judge Tall would find objectionable."

Mary retrieved a large enough package of chicken breasts to accommodate the dinner for four, which in her mind was two more than she preferred. "There's plenty she finds objectionable, but I think I can put something together," she said under her breath. When she had returned to the counter, she said, "You know I'm saving my money to build a roof garden. Then I can grow my own produce and better manage rainwater runoff." Mary put Sadie's order together and bagged it.

"How'd you become acquainted with Judge Tall? She didn't live here back when you lived in Whistler. I heard she was run out of a town on the North Dakota border under suspicion that she ran the Swedish Mafia."

"Gospel truth," Win squawked from his cage.

"She was on the search committee that interviewed and hired me for my new position. I'd never heard of her before then, but after I met her, I read her books of course. And, well, like I said, I had a legal question for her."

"I wonder if she's hearing this request by Big Bottom Foods to prohibit use of the town's barbeque sauce recipe at Carnival?"

"I'm so tired of hearing about Big Bottom Foods and the Carnival. It has nothing to do with me really." Sadie fumbled with her purse. "I don't know what case she's hearing. She was busy at court yesterday and had some ruling to give today, but

I don't know any details. She's very ethical about not disclosing private and confidential information."

"Yeah, unless she's working her other job as proofreader and gossip columnist for the paper. Your dinner, the guests, and even the menu may appear in the *Whistler Tribune* along with news of who visited whom for the weekend, notable wedding anniversaries, and holy communions. Judge Tall tells all." Mary knew she sounded catty and jealous. It was difficult for her to hear in what high esteem Sadie held the judge. She had wanted to be the sole recipient of Sadie's adoration since she met her.

"Well, the dinner is to be held at the judge's house so I suppose she can write anything about it that she wants."

"I *would* like to see her house and gardens." Mary had only ever driven past the Tall place and never driven up the long, tarred driveway to the judge's lair. She'd never seen the house and gardens up close. She certainly had never been inside. She felt a sense of prohibition about approaching the place not entirely unlike the thought of risking being shot by Martin Latiskee.

"I heard she has about every kind of fruit tree and flower that would grow in zone four. Maybe that's why she picks over my vegetables like I may have fertilized them from my own toilet." Mary bought a large variety of local, organic produce. She wanted to see the judge's garden patch and know if the house and yard were as impressive as their roadside appeal suggested.

"We're not exactly friends—more like occasional sparring partners and I come away with most of the bruises. Judge Tall comes into my store every week and although she's had little praise for my produce, she purchases my butter in quantities that would scare you. I pity her arteries. Perhaps she is practicing butter sculpting to enter at the state fair."

"Maybe she's doing a butter bust of your big head." Sadie laughed.

"She depletes my dried beef with regularity and before the holidays she inevitably hounds me about whether I've ordered that godforsaken excuse for nourishment, lutefisk. That recipe is an abomination to fish everywhere. I tell her it's been banned by the Food and Drug Administration just to watch disgust rise up from her wrinkled neck to the silver hair she has 'fixed' every week at the beauty shop across the street." Mary started to add a bouquet of flowers to Sadie's order, but aborted the effort since Judge Tall had much revered gardens. "She sells Avon too. Avon. God, I wonder if she took up selling it to blot out the stench of the lutefisk."

"You're awful. You of all people should have an appreciation for exotic cuisine."

"I'm not awful and I do appreciate exotic cuisine. Aged fish soaked in lye is not exotic cuisine. I understand aged cheese and have known intimately aged wine and whiskey, but lutefisk? That's more of a biological weapon than an entrée. She always tries to leave an Avon book with me—like I have need for soap on a rope, lipstick, or men's cologne in bottles shaped like cowboys on horseback." Mary realized she had gone on at some length in a mostly negative fashion. She added, "She smells nice. I'll give her that."

"I should think you'd be interested in something beyond this grocery store and the Carnival." Sadie looked at Mary like she was waiting for a response.

Mary could have said, wanted to say, wished to hell in retrospect she'd said, "I'm interested in you." Instead she said, "I'm looking at adding a roof garden."

"Well, I suppose that's something." Sadie gathered up her bag of groceries.

"Judge Tall smells nice."

"Dinner is tonight at six p.m. at the judge's home. Come over or don't come. It's your decision. Do I need to buy beer for you to show up?"

Stab to the heart. Gunshot to the temple.

"No, unless Judge Tall is a boozer. No beer for me." She wanted to add that she hadn't had a drink in five years, but she knew it wasn't the time to tell that story. It saddened her to know that Sadie expected her to be the same.

"Well, maybe I'll see you then. There's something I need to ask you."

Mary looked up expectantly. "Oh?"

"Never mind; it can wait until I see you later." Sadie marched out of the store without smiling or even paying for her groceries. Mary watched Sadie through the store window as she hurriedly untied the Muffin sequel and walked away, lugging her groceries in a canvas bag. Mary stood there feeling alien in her own store. Disappointment surfaced like a buoy she'd been attempting to hold below the surface of the water. She had managed to irritate Sadie even as Sadie asked her over for dinner.

On the positive side—she sifted through the memory of the encounter looking for a positive side—she could say that they still sparked high emotion in one another. She hoped soon she could incite something in the pleasant range, but she had her doubts.

Sarah and Jimmy returned from their pseudo break. Sarah was laughing at something Jimmy had said.

"It's true," he said. "The hairs in his ears are so long that she can use them for a comb over and Bobby told me that Coach Mullen's wife has to shave his back every week or wiry stuff pokes out his shirt."

"Oh, that's gross." Sarah sat on her stool, put her hand to her belly, and smiled at Jimmy.

"It's just biology like you always talk about." Jimmy conscientiously found the next thing needing his attention. He refilled the shelf with paper grocery bags.

"God, it feels good to laugh about something instead of just feeling awful," Sarah said.

"Amen to that." Sarah's laugh was music to Mary, and she thought perhaps it had a little to do with Sarah's growing connection to Jimmy. For once her head wasn't in a biology book or SAT test preparation workbook. Sarah Hanley apparently thought about college and read so much about microorganisms that the information dropped out of her mouth in everyday conversation as if the unseeable specks of the universe were of general interest and as engaging as weather and high school sports. Mary found the habit dear especially because Sarah appreciated Win and Mary was feeling a growing affection for Sarah as well.

"Mary, did you know that some researchers think crows developed like mammals did?"

"I'm not surprised. It has always seemed to me that Win has more in common with people than with reptiles or insects. He talks, he makes collections—oh, that reminds me, do you think you narrowed down the location of his other hiding spots?"

"We followed him as best we could, considering he flies and we don't. He went to Lake Pepin first and then to the park. I wasn't fast enough to see where he fiddled around in either place." Jimmy hung his head.

Sarah touched Jimmy's arm. "Of course, this was just our first attempt." Sarah looked at Mary and then at him. "I don't think it would hurt to try this again, maybe every day. As you probably know, crows and ravens have big brains compared to their body size and their forebrain is impressive. They hide things with an awareness that some other creature may be watching them with nefarious intent."

"Some people say birds are stupid." Mary directed this comment in Win's direction.

Win promptly said, "Bullshit!"

Mary looked over at Win and said, "I believe that birds are very intelligent and even use tools."

Win said, "Gospel truth."

Sarah looked at Mary and then again at Win. "Wait a minute. How'd you teach him to do that?"

Mary didn't answer Sarah but smiled at Win. "Well, I better check the collection spot I know about. He pretends to hide it in the beverage aisle, but he really stashes it in the back room. See you later." Mary exited into the back room.

More and more Mary found herself left with little to do beyond the bookkeeping and wholesale ordering. As she had bragged to Sadie, she allowed Sarah and Jimmy to work additional hours as long as they had cleared it with their parents. She had grown accustomed to having the two of them around the store. They became characters in the stories in her mind. She wondered what they thought, liked to eat, and if they liked it at the store.

Even as she thumbed through the bits and bobs Win had collected and stashed in his cache by the potato bin—a few pop tops, several twist ties, a faded red, paper poppy, and a torn corner of paper that read "onion flakes"—Mary remained preoccupied with Sadie being in town and what help she needed from Mary. *Sponge bath?* Then Mary remembered the dinner was at the judge's home.

Although Win's stash meant nothing to Mary, she listed the items on a small notepad she kept in her pocket for the increasing number of things she needed to jot down to remember. She put the detritus back in Win's hiding spot and prepared herself for dinner with Sadie and Judge Tall.

CHAPTER THIRTEEN

Judge Not, Lest Ye Be Judged

The drive to Little Swan Lake was one of Mary's favorite trips. It reminded her of the times her father would suggest a drive in the country. He pointed to farmsteads he recognized and referred to some places by the names of their past owners: the old Truog Place, Czech's, the Dzieweczynski place, Shrups, Dreckman's, Blood's house, Hickman's place, and Lambrecht property. She drove on roads that didn't have numbers but other more colorful names like Pillsbury Road and the Bunny Trail.

Her father had been a hunter. He had hunted ducks, squirrels, and deer. He loved to drive at dusk and point out the deer along the seam of the fields and woods. He marveled at their beauty in summer and in fall shot them with a rifle and had the locker plant dress them out for the sale of venison chops, roasts, and sausage in the store.

The driveway to the Tall place was long but paved. The lawn sloped off from the drive to flatter grounds with groves of trees and gardens. The outbuildings matched the architecture and paint of the main house as if they'd been purchased in a set.

Mary parked her truck between the judge's Chevy Blazer and a Subaru station wagon that must be Sadie's.

"Come in, come in!" Judge Tall held the storm door open and waved Mary into the house. "Sadie is in the kitchen cooking dinner." She led Mary through the porch.

The house was bigger than it appeared from the outside. Immediately, Mary was aware of the scent of the house. It smelled clean and good. Certainly, she detected the aroma of roasting chicken, but there were other notes on the scale, something pleasant. *Avon? Shit.* It had to be the products the woman peddled. Maybe Mary needed something from Avon for her store. She nearly slapped herself at the thought.

The large hutch that flanked the far wall of the dining room immediately grabbed visual and aural attention. It shook with their every footstep. China and porcelain cup sets rattled against each other on the shelves like someone playing the high notes on a piano. The rectangular dining room table was large, wooden with clean lines, and sat below the double sashed windows. Mary bet that somewhere Judge Tall had enough leaves for that table that it would have covered the room and been wide and long enough to stand on to paint the ceiling.

A rhythmic tick brought Mary's eyes to the grandmother clock with its butter plate-sized pendulum bob swinging side-to-side, marking time. It hung on the wall between the front door and the doorway of the living room. A wooden secretary stood like an open mouth against the adjacent wall. A small writing desk with a center drawer and four small side drawers was dwarfed by the hutch and by Judge Tall.

That was apparently where the judge did some of her newspaper writing and bookkeeping. Pens and journals covered the surface of the desk. A manual typewriter, not an electric one or a computer, stood on a small, black, metal table near the desk. Nothing was easy, but most things were sturdy and functional when it came to Judge Tall.

Mary passed through the dining room, sneaking a glance into a downstairs bedroom and hallway into what was perhaps the bathroom and another bedroom. She entered the kitchen.

The small yellow room shone with cheerfulness and cleanliness. White metal cabinets hung on the east wall. A small rectangular Formica table was set for three—still one too many in Mary's estimation. The uneven floor creaked and its linoleum skin made a crinkly sound under her feet. There was no dust, no crumbs, no grease, and had the table not been overlaid with place settings and serving bowls Mary would have concluded that Judge Tall either never used the room, which she knew was ridiculous considering the amount of butter she bought, or maybe that there was a drain in the floor allowing her to hose the dust and food particles away each night.

A humming emanated from a massive white, top-freezer refrigerator next to a free-standing, white enamel stove—this too, spotless. Sadie had her head in the oven checking the chicken. Judge Tall peeked into a Crock-pot and then slapped a quarter cup of butter on to the top of the mashed potatoes warming there. Mary thought maybe the old bird wasn't so awful after all.

"Look around if you want," said Judge Tall, waving toward the backyard with her spoon. "Dinner is almost ready. Sadie has done the lion's share of the work. I just need to put together a fresh salad."

Here it comes. She's going to insult my vegetables. But Judge Tall didn't say any more. She brandished a big knife and began slicing carrots.

The kitchen emptied into a small back porch with a chest freezer and trapdoor for what Mary assumed was a basement containing the furnace, water heater, and possibly a torture chamber. The jewel of the property lay beyond the back porch.

"Holy mother of God!" Judge Tall had a vast, sprawling three-season porch that flanked that entire side of the house. The walls were paneled in knotty pine and screened windows looked out on all sides. A deck wrapped around all three sides of the porch and Mary speculated that the smaller, adjacent screened porch was a potting shed that Mary imagined had been repurposed for cleaning fish. Mary wanted to move into the house immediately after moving Judge Tall out.

Off through the leaves of mature oaks, birch, and maples Mary could see the still surface of Little Swan Lake. The yard closer to the house was dotted with more gardens than Mary had ever seen outside of an arboretum. Round gardens, rectangular gardens, flower gardens, and vegetable gardens. Why in the hell did the old woman bust Mary's chops about her produce when the old bird grew her own? She couldn't be mad. She was too impressed by the fountains and rain gardens, gardens of ornamental grasses, bushes and berries, bird feeders and bird baths. Judge Tall had them all surrounding her house like her own Eden.

For a moment Mary wondered if the woman had ever availed herself of the beauty and privacy of the place to have a sexual tryst in the yard. Mary slapped herself for the notion but filed the idea away under experiences to consider should the judge need a housesitter.

Once Mary could tear her eyes away from the gardens and lake view, she returned to the kitchen. Judge Tall was holding court and appeared to be scolding Sadie about something. "I just don't understand why'd you go there."

"Go where? Boy, if I lived here, I wouldn't want to go anywhere. Judge Tall, would you marry me?" Mary asked.

"I'd certainly perform the ceremony if I were marrying you to someone else." Judge Tall gave Mary the stink eye as she placed a bowl of salad on the table.

"Oh, it's nothing. I can explain it after dinner." Sadie placed a platter of baked chicken breasts on the table. She then unplugged the Crock-pot and brought the entire appliance to the table. "I remember how you love potatoes."

Muffin suddenly appeared from the other room. The dog barked and jumped on Mary for attention. She rubbed the dog's ears as she distractedly took in the kitchen and the two women fussing over dinner and apparently something else they hadn't found the courage to say.

Judge Tall and Sadie glanced back and forth at each other. Mary studied them like they were a math problem on a blackboard.

Finally, Judge Tall said, "You might as well tell her. The story doesn't get any prettier."

"Tell me what?" Mary's mind raced with fantastical ideas, but her musings didn't even approach the story line that followed.

"I was at Lake Pepin." Sadie stared at her hands in her lap like a guilty child.

"Yeah, so? I don't understand. It's a public landing. You can go there any time you want."

"I was at the lake the day those two men died."

Don't panic. There's a reasonable explanation. "Oh. Why were you at the lake?"

"That's what I said," Judge Tall interjected. "Why anyone would spend time at that green swamp when you're just a couple miles from pristine Little Swan is beyond me." The judge filled her plate—two thirds with potatoes. "Tell her about your necklace."

"What necklace?" Mary stopped herself. She took a breath. "Tell me what happened. It's okay. I'll help you anyway I can."

"Thank you." Sadie began her story. "I'd been working at the school all afternoon and into the evening. There's no air conditioning in that office. It's hot and stuffy. Anyway, on my walk home I stopped at the lake just before dusk to get some air, think, and maybe reminisce about my time in Whistler." Her face reddened.

Mary wondered if Sadie visited the same intimate memories Mary had.

"I felt like the lake called to me through the windows of the school. Is that nuts?" Sadie asked.

"Probably. Most people know you don't call anybody anymore, you text."

Sadie continued. "I stopped there before returning home that night."

"Okay, how does that connect with Buddy and the other guy?"

"That's what's so weird. I was standing at the end of the dock and Buddy showed up. He said something about my big butt and then he got way too close. He asked, "Do you have it?""

"Have what?" Mary asked.

"I don't know. I was fuming over the comment about my butt. Do you think my butt looks big?"

Judge Tall nudged Sadie's arm. "Maybe you can look for that salve another time."

"Oh, yes. When I told him that I didn't know what he was talking about, he got angry and grabbed my arm."

"Did he hurt you?" Mary stood up.

"No, but he talked like he was rabid. I didn't catch most of it. He said something about idiots who worked all their lives for nothing but a bad back and inadequate pension. He said something about soon having a family to think about."

"What do you suppose he meant by that?" Mary felt an itch or tickle in her brain like there was something she should remember.

"I don't know, and I didn't ask for details."

"Were you scared he was going to hurt you?" Mary sat down again but leaned closer to Sadie.

"Yes, I guess I was. I saw Judge Tall's sister, Clara, driving by and I waved to her. I remember thinking 'I hope she stops.' She didn't. I don't know. Maybe she didn't even see me or recognize me." Sadie turned to Judge Tall, "I hate to say it, but I think she is slipping cognitively. Her memory is shot."

"I know, dear. That's a whole other kettle of fish." Judge Tall turned to Mary. "When the sheriff was asking about people who might have seen something at the lake Clara called him and told him she saw Sadie with Buddy." Judge Tall took another scoop of potatoes and more butter.

"It's okay." Sadie touched Judge Tall's hand. "She was only doing what she thought was right. Anyway, in my struggle to get past Buddy on the dock my necklace broke and dropped into the water."

"Oh, Sadie. Was it the one…? I'm so sorry." Mary wanted to ask her why she hadn't come to the store after but kept that question to herself.

"I was so angry at his comment and losing my necklace that I just pushed him with every ounce of strength I had." She playacted the motion. "He fell in the water and I left. I didn't look for my necklace." She sighed and looked at her lap.

"The next day I learned he'd been found dead and I was worried that I might have killed him. I knew I had pushed him into the shallow water, but I thought what if he hit his head? Maybe he drowned because of me. But then I read the sheriff's lips saying he was shot. It doesn't make sense."

"So you didn't shoot him?" Mary said.

Sadie punched Mary's arm. "Don't even joke about such a thing."

"My point is that after you left, he got out of the water and somebody shot him. Wow, Buddy had an incredibly bad day."

"I guess. It seems highly unlikely that it happened at the same time. I don't remember hearing a gunshot. I wish I knew who did it."

"Don't we all." Mary scratched her head. "What about Kavanaugh? What do you know about him?"

"It's a long story and I will tell you someday. First, we need to find that necklace." Sadie put her hand on Mary's wrist. Mary wondered if the judge would perform the wedding ceremony she had mentioned right then. Still, she was having trouble taking it all in.

"I have to know you will help me find the necklace. Nobody'd think anything of you being down by that dock."

"You can't hardly see any fish now. Lake's got so weedy. Shore fishing is no good." Mary was prepared to go on at some length, more from the daze she was in than any current interest in talking about fishing.

Sadie interrupted. "Just pretend you're fishing then. Don't you see? If they find that necklace, it leads back to me."

Mary knew. She also knew that the necklace led back to her as well. Both of their initials were engraved in the soft, yellow gold of the pendant heart. She had given that necklace to Sadie a million years ago when they both said they loved each other. "Don't worry, I'll find it."

Judge Amanda Tall, who Mary thought of now as "Commanda," brought her fist down on the table. "Now that

that's settled, let's eat." She ignored the fact she had been eating since they first sat down.

"Judge, you're an officer of the court. How can you be a party to this discussion?" Mary asked.

"Fiddlesticks. I know Sadie wouldn't kill a fly. The sheriff already knows she was there, and he'll get her statement. Retrieving that necklace doesn't mean diddly squat. Besides, I hear civil suits. Speaking of which, it's public record, but I heard the request for an injunction on use of that barbeque sauce recipe. I gave my ruling this morning."

"What did you rule?"

"I didn't. I scheduled an evidentiary hearing." Judge Tall paused. She looked at Mary and smiled with just the corners of her mouth raised and no teeth showing. Her eyes sparkled. "I'll hear evidence from both sides the first week of August."

"You wily jurist." Mary shook her head and grinned.

"Thank you. I'll take that as a compliment."

"What? What does all this mean?" Sadie asked.

"The Carnival will be over before that evidentiary hearing so Big Bottom Foods can't stop Whistler from using the barbeque recipe. There will be barbequed chicken at the Carnival. The Carnival is safe this year for sure." Mary rose up and kissed Judge Tall on the lips. "Well, that is if any volunteers sign up to help."

Judge Tall rubbed her lips with a cloth napkin like she was making an angry correction before she spoke again. "In the meantime, unless someone produces that certified copy of the recipe or proof that the recipe has been legally sold, it will be like nothing happened until that hearing. The dead bodies, however, are another matter of course. Shame if the wrong person is accused." She glared at Mary over her spoon of potatoes.

Mary sighed, "I'll help you look for the necklace tomorrow morning before Buddy's funeral."

Sadie squeezed her hand. "Thank you. Pick me up when you are ready to go over there."

CHAPTER FOURTEEN

Laid to Rest

The next day when Mary came down from her apartment, she found Sarah already at the counter in the front of the store. It was a half-hour before opening.

"I hope you don't mind that I used my key and came in early." Sarah emptied the bank bag into the till.

If Mary remembered correctly Sarah was wearing the same clothes as she had the day before. An alarm went off in Mary's head, one that she didn't have time to address completely that morning. She filed the information.

"Good morning. You being here early or late is no problem for me. Do you mind watching the store on your own? Jimmy was checking with his mom about coming in at ten so that you can go to the funeral. Just close the store if he can't work or you decide to go to the funeral together."

"Would you mind if I eat breakfast here today? I'll pay for it."

Mary wished she had time to stay and cook for the girl. She would fatten Sarah up with bacon, eggs, sausage, pancakes, and hash browns.

"That's fine, Sarah." Another, louder alarm sounded in Mary's head but before she could better assess a strategy, she said, "You know, the back room has a bathroom and kind of a guest room area if a guest didn't mind sharing with boxes upon boxes of cereal, cat food, canned goods, and paper products. There's even a small refrigerator by the twin-size bed. The dresser isn't very big, but if you ever need to keep a few things here at the store, you're welcome."

Since Sarah didn't interrupt and insist that she couldn't on her life accept such accommodations, Mary continued. "Take some toiletries and store them back there in case you need them when you're working and don't have them with you. There's plenty of space in this building. You can sleep here if you're too tired to go home."

The words fell from Mary's mouth unexpected and fast like a slip on an icy sidewalk. She took inventory of herself after she said it—nothing broken or soiled. She didn't retract the invite.

Sarah looked at Mary and didn't speak right away.

"You don't have to use any of it, of course." Mary wondered if she had moved too quickly and spooked the girl. "I'm not trying to boss you, just offering. You put in a lot of hours here and sometimes it might be nice to have some things of your own to freshen up. No pressure."

Sarah unlocked the front door and flipped the sign to Open. "Okay. Thank you, Mary."

Before either Sarah or Mary could talk anymore the store door opened and Mayor Carl entered. He was all aflutter, red-faced and perspiring.

"Did you hear? Whistler's still buzzing. The Carnival will proceed as planned. Evidentiary hearing is set for August. Huh, if that don't beat all. Not only that, it was officially announced that the Kavanaugh man died of natural consequences—a heart attack. There weren't two murders—if Buddy was even murdered. See, things work out."

"I don't know what else you'd call being shot in the neck. It sure looks like somebody murdered Buddy." Sarah blinked away tears.

"Well, Mayor Carl, that is good news. I love the Carnival." Mary took some new gloves from the gardening shelf and grabbed an additional pair for Sadie. "I see you left your sidearm at home. I, for one, appreciate the gesture."

Mayor Carl touched his belly, ran his fingers up and down the lapels of his suit, and mumbled something Mary didn't catch.

"The awful news is that they're planning to drag the lake. Looking for a gun. They're cordoning off the crime scene at ten." Mayor Carl glanced at his watch. "And dragging right after." He rocked back and forth on the heels of his dress shoes and fingered his suspenders. "Damn waste of time if you want to know. And this being almost Carnival week. That carnival outfit is due any minute."

"What's got the sheriff thinking the gun's in the lake?" Mary asked.

"Who knows? Say, you got any of them skin-on wieners?"

"Yep, back with the rest of the meats, $5.99 a pound and one joke for every two pounds purchased."

"You can keep your jokes, but I will take a half pound of them wieners. No need to wrap 'em, I'll just put them in my pocket here."

"Okay. Watch out for tall dogs and short dogs with a good vertical jump. You're a walking temptation, Mayor Carl." Mary fetched a half pound of wieners from the cool case. "Say, what do you make of the missing barbeque recipe?"

Mayor Carl's face bloomed purple splotches. "What makes you ask me that? You think I can't take care of such a thing?" He waved his arms, forgetting he'd been grasping his elastic suspenders. He snapped his own man boobs. "You think I'd be careless with such a valuable town treasure? Well, you just keep your hot dogs—probably made out of lips, ears, and beaks anyhow. I'll get me something at the convenience store." He stomped out of the store.

"What's with Mayor Carl? His face looks like a big bruise." Sarah restocked the paper sacks.

"He was on the precipice of purchasing all beef wieners when he thought better of it, citing that they may contain beaks. Then he left the store. I think this murder happening and happening so close to Carnival weekend has people pretty rattled."

"I heard him say that they are dragging Lake Pepin. Who knows what else they might find in there?"

With any luck they'll find less than they would have.

CHAPTER FIFTEEN

Lost and Found and Lost Again

Mary grabbed her fishing pole and a rake and went out the back door. She marched down the alley and crossed the street to the sidewalk that led to Sadie's apartment.

"You look like half of a new American Gothic," Sadie said as she answered the door to Mary.

"I feel more like an extra in a Hitchcock film. I need you to give me some idea where to look for your necklace."

"Let me change my shoes. I'll come with you." Sadie ran back up the stairs but didn't ask Mary up.

The idea of Sadie accompanying her to the lake pleased Mary, but the circumstances gave her pause. She waited outside, swaying from foot to foot, trying to look nonchalant. She absentmindedly checked the pockets on her fishing vest. She found a dusty cherry Lifesaver and some mints. She put the mints in her mouth. She felt more conspicuous by the minute. She found herself offering explanations to passersby and to folks who didn't ask a thing and who were on the other side of the street anyway. "I'm going fishing, at the lake, Lake Pepin. Might as well rake some while I'm there. Probably no fish biting."

"Who are you talking to?" Sadie locked the outside door to the stairway of her apartment.

"Well, plenty of people are wondering about these goings-on. I explained that I'm going fishing."

"It's pretty obvious you're going fishing, Mary."

"I don't usually bring a rake along."

"That's a fair point, but I doubt anybody even notices your 'goings-on.'"

That statement hurt Mary somewhere in her chest, but she couldn't argue the point. "Let's walk by the St. John's Catholic Church and then cut over along the horse arena."

"We could drive."

"Nah, that would be too suspicious." Mary looked both ways before she crossed the street.

Sadie followed. "At least if we drove you could hide the rake."

"I think it would be more suspicious if folks saw me driving that short ways to the lake than me sporting a fishing pole and a rake. I could be wrong."

"Did you, Mary Caine, just admit you could be wrong about something? Mark the calendars folks! Check the temperature in hell. It may have frozen over."

"Do you want my help or not?"

"I do."

"Then stop insulting me. We need to get a move on. Mayor Carl told me they are dragging the lake today looking for the gun. It's due to be cordoned off as a crime scene again."

As they walked in the taller grasses beside the road grasshoppers and other bugs lit from the weeds into the air like tiny quail.

"Mary, maybe we can't go there. Maybe we'd look more suspicious. Maybe there's that yellow tape with the black writing on it." Sadie stopped dead in her tracks.

Mary motioned for her to keep moving. "I've had so much experience with red tape that yellow tape doesn't intimidate me at all. Besides, they're not taping until ten. We'll be done before that and that necklace doesn't take any evidence away from who killed Buddy. You heard Judge Tall. She can write us a note if we get into trouble—kind of a Get Out of Jail free card."

"You can joke. No one is suspecting you." Sadie caught up to Mary. "So, you do believe me that I ran into him, but I didn't kill him?"

"Of course, I believe you. By the way, to answer your question from last night, no, your butt doesn't look big." Sadie didn't say anything, but she smiled.

"I can't for the life of me imagine why you'd kill anybody or have anything to do with Big Bottom Foods."

Sadie didn't say anything but smiled like she'd just been caught in something.

Oh, Christ on a Harley. "You don't have anything to do with Big Bottom Foods, do you?"

"Do you think I could have killed McConnell?"

"Of course not. I heard today that he died of natural causes. Besides, you don't even know…wait, did you just call him McConnell?"

Tell me you don't know McConnell Kavanaugh.

Sadie looked away from Mary.

"You don't have a connection to Kavanaugh, do you?" Mary stopped walking.

Sadie continued walking. "Yes, I met him when I was taking some business classes before I moved here."

"Oh crap." Mary caught up to Sadie.

"Now listen. It isn't as bad as you think."

"Did you tell Kavanaugh about the barbeque recipe?"

"It may have come up in conversation." Sadie walked faster.

"Oh, two scoops of crap."

"Quit saying that. I didn't hurt that man or Buddy either, but it might look like I had something to do with it." Sadie stopped, eyes wide as she looked at Mary. "I was planning to tell you."

"I don't think I want to know."

"He was supposed to call me if his wholesale food conglomerate was interested in buying the barbeque sauce recipe. I didn't know it was Big Bottom until later and I didn't know he was in town. I had planned to set up a meeting between him and someone from the Lions Club."

"Why would *you* set up a meeting with him and someone from the Lions Club?" Mary grew more and more confused and could feel herself moving toward angry at breakneck speed. She wished for a nanosecond she were still drinking to numb the disappointment she sensed encompassing her life.

"You're 'the teacher.' God damn it." Mary stepped away. She couldn't believe what she was hearing or thinking. "Natvig, Gessell, Tepley, Primus, Oven, Olson, Johnson, Nelson, Peterson, Thieschafer, Tepley, Beseman, Berge, Borgert, Golombecki, Swisher, VanNorman, and Mayor Carl were in my store and they talked about a rumor that a teacher was involved in the plan to sell the recipe. Shit, shit, shit."

This wasn't how it was supposed to be. Sadie had returned to Whistler. They were supposed to get back together, be lovers. Life partners. Not partners in crime.

She wracked her brain for another way to say it but kept coming back to the same harsh words. "Sadie, God damn it. It wasn't your place to broker anything about the Carnival and definitely not secretly. Do you know what trouble you've started?"

Sadie looked like she'd been slapped. "It's not like I gave him the recipe."

"The certified recipe is still missing."

"Well, I don't have it." Sadie glared at her. "You don't think I have it, do you? Or the check?"

"No, of course not." She shot her a quick glance. "You don't, do you? I'm sorry, Sadie. I'm sure your intentions were good. You can't control what other people might do when they see a chance to make a quick buck. To think that they almost canceled the Carnival."

"The Carnival. Of course, what could be more important than the Carnival? You don't even seem worried that I may be a suspect in a murder."

They had reached the lake and an impasse.

Mary knew Sadie was probably embarrassed about Mary calling her out for talking about selling the barbeque recipe. She was embarrassed that it was necessary. Maybe Sadie felt the sting of being an outsider yet again since she wasn't born and raised in Whistler. People could be considered "new" for decades. Mary couldn't change that reality and it would now be compounded by this high treason.

She lowered her fishing pole and rake to the grass. She walked out onto the dock, scanning the shallows. "Of course I'm worried about you being suspected of murder and I don't for the life of me think you killed anyone." She pivoted to a new area of conversation. "The lake is calm."

"At least there's calm somewhere. I'm a wreck. I shouldn't have come back."

"Don't say that. It's good you're here." Mary went to her knees, looking between the slats of the dock into the water.

"I thought I could do this, but I can't."

"I'll find the necklace. I promise."

"I'm not talking about the necklace," Sadie shouted. Mary looked up. "I shouldn't have come back to Whistler."

Mary got to her feet again slowly but still feeling wobbly—like she might fall into the water herself.

"I have been lying to myself that I'm over being angry at you. I'm not. I am still royally peeved. You're a coward, Mary Caine."

"That's a bit harsh. I admit I'm nervous about being down here disturbing a crime scene, but I don't know that it makes me a coward."

"I'm not talking about being here at the dock. You were a coward all those years ago when we were together, when we could have stayed together."

The words hit Mary like a punch. She swallowed hard and hoped she wouldn't begin crying.

Sadie approached Mary on the dock. Her face was flushed and there were tears in her eyes. She shook her head side-to-side. "You were a coward long before Buddy Latiskee was even born. You were a coward when we could have had a life together."

"So this isn't about what happened at the lake or you trying to sell the barbeque recipe? You're angry about what happened."

"What happened? Is that some sort of euphemism? Can't you just bring yourself to say that you refused to go away with me all those years ago?"

"Okay. You are still angry with me for not leaving Whistler with you."

"Yes, I am. Go ahead, make your argument about why I shouldn't be. List all the things that you always do for the reason you don't live your own life. Your father, the store, your mother leaving you and your father when you were young, your drinking."

Mary was tired of making her arguments and had pretty much given up the practice since finding AA. "I don't argue, and I don't like your tone."

"Tough s-h-i-t!" Sadie again spelled her swear word.

"You can say those hateful things to me, but you stifle yourself from saying 'shit.'" Mary raked through her hair with her hands. "Not being with you made me want to scream every swear word I could think of. I wanted to learn six additional languages, so I could shout those words too."

"Screw the necklace. What does it matter?" Sadie turned to leave the dock. "I guess we have irreconcilable differences."

"That's better than unrecognizable differences, I suppose." Mary waited a beat. "What good would it have done had I went with you? You married Graham." The words, like a baited hook cast from Mary's fishing rod, reeled Sadie back in.

"That's your argument?" Sadie turned back to Mary. "I would have met and married Graham anyway? Why couldn't the two of us—you and me—have been happy together? And don't tell me it was because I wouldn't stay in Whistler."

Mary was disoriented. She thought she might fall down. She tried to say what she knew was true and real. "I couldn't compete with the life you could have if you left." She fell to her knees on the dock. She hoped she'd be able to stand up again.

"How do you know that?" Sadie was crying now.

"I know," Mary said, but she honestly didn't know anything more than what was in her head and heart. She cried too.

"You weren't even willing to try. I thought you were so brave that first night you told me that your father was being charming in order to get you to date me. I thought, man, oh man this woman has balls. Yes, I used the word balls." Sadie walked closer but didn't go onto the dock. "All those dinners we had, talks, and then the lovemaking. I thought this woman knows what she wants and I'm part of it. Thank God in heaven that I am a part of it."

Mary sobbed. Tears and snot ran down her face onto her neck and shirt faster than she could wipe them away with her sleeve. In a strangled voice she weakly said, "Stop."

"You didn't think a life with me was worth trying for. That's what hurts the most. If you would have just left with me, I would have known we were real, not just hidden figures only together in the dark." Sadie turned on her heels and walked off the dock.

Bob Barker groaned like he sensed the discord.

"Shut up, Bob." Mary watched Sadie receding from the landing. She had not imagined telling Sadie about her recovery in a shouting match, but she felt like she didn't have another choice. She shouted, "Sadie, I knew I couldn't compete with the life you could have because I was drinking. I was a drunk then and for years after. I'm still an alcoholic, but I'm not drinking anymore."

Sadie slowed. It seemed like she was solving a math problem in her head. Finally, she turned back to Mary and said, "Why wasn't a life with me enough for you to get sober back then?"

Mary didn't answer.

Then Sadie moved away from the lake.

Stricken by Sadie's words, Mary bowed her head in shame and regret. How could she explain that getting sober wasn't about others not being enough? Her sobriety came from the realization that she was an insane drunk and that only God could remove her compulsion to drink and her defects of character. Her self-will hadn't worked and neither did others' expectations of her or her expectations of others.

She didn't know how to say all that. She maybe would have tried, but something in the shallows below the dock caught her eye. "Wait!" she shouted to Sadie and scrambled into the water, shoes and all. Win swooped by, a little too close to Mary's head for her way of thinking. "Hey, watch it!"

By this time, Sadie was running from the lakeside. If she heard Mary's calls, she didn't look back.

Win flew by again, mumbling and swearing. Mary ducked down and then knelt in the water, peering between the wooden slats of the dock. Something shiny was caught on a bolt securing the dock leg to the diagonal truss. She reached under the dock, feeling the soft resistance of spider webs across the back of her hand. She stretched and just barely reached it with the tips of her fingers, but the necklace's suspension was so precarious that it fell into the water and slithered like a silver eel into the muck below. Shit.

She dug her knees deeper into the lake bottom and strained to the spot where the chain had fallen. Her reach was inches short. She took a breath, put her face in the water, and ducked her head under the dock. The smell of the murky water was both disgusting and comfortingly familiar to Mary. She raked her hands through silt. She collected everything she snagged and swished her hands in the water to free the booty from the stringy weeds and mud as she extricated herself from under the dock. Mary spit out the tepid water, wiped her nose and eyes. "I'm too old for this shit," she said to the empty shoreline.

Win landed on the dock just a few feet from Mary.

What the hell? Mary looked into her hand and found Sadie's necklace. She lifted it into the sunlight.

Win took flight again. "Mine," he said just before he plucked the necklace like a berry from Mary's hand.

"What are you talking about? You crazy bird. Give that back!" She sloshed drunkenly out of the shallow water, tripping once.

Bob Barker barked at Win. Mary cussed at Win. Win flew away.

Mary hoped Win was returning to the store or that he would drop Sadie's necklace on Sadie's head. She worried that Win would stuff his booty into one of the suspected hiding spots on the map Sarah and Jimmy were constructing. She'd get that necklace back. The bird didn't know who he was dealing with when it came to a quest that Mary had taken on for Sadie.

Sadie. Would she ever talk to Mary again?

Mary was soaked and beginning to feel cold even though the day was hot and humid. She picked up her fishing gear and rake. As she walked back to the store, leaving wet footprints and making a squishy sound with every step, she examined the other items she'd found nested in lake pulp: a large lead sinker, a rusted daredevil, and a newish, silver cylinder. When Mary turned it on end she read, *Beyond Color Revenge*.

"Huh, somebody lost their Avon lipstick." She examined the color and showed it to Bob Barker, who walked at her side back to the store.

CHAPTER SIXTEEN

I Remember You

Mary entered the store through the back, tracking water and lake muck onto the floor she had never scrubbed and rarely swept. She alternated stern words at Sadie and cuss words at Win under her breath. Bob Barker came in like a reasonable pet. She held the door a few minutes longer, hoping that thieving bird would arrive with the necklace. He didn't. Mary slammed the back door. She checked Win's cache by the potatoes. Nothing new except a few more scraps of white paper she didn't bother to examine. "Damn it." She went up to her apartment.

"Bob, I don't care if that feathered thief of a bird stays out all night." She did care, of course, and worried that the unpredictable bird might deposit Sadie's necklace someplace Mary hadn't found before or worse yet on the sheriff's head. She paced, removed her wet clothes, vented all this to Bob Barker, who snored as he slept on the floor, exhausted from the walk to the lake. He ignored her.

"Are you kidding me? Now even my dog doesn't listen to me."

Once Mary had showered and changed into dry clothes, she moved from room to room like she had left something there, all the time repeating in her head, "I found the necklace. It's not my fault that Win took it."

Did it matter that it was no longer in her possession? There was no way that necklace would make it into the hands of law enforcement, she told herself. Although, she had to admit there were no guarantees about what Win would do with his booty.

Could she approach Sadie while Sadie was so angry? Could she go to her after Sadie had called her a coward? Could she go to her when she knew Sadie was connected somehow to McConnell Kavanaugh? She wasn't sure.

After more purposeless walking and mental calisthenics that produced no answers only a splitting headache, Mary dropped to her knees and prayed the Serenity Prayer. It was her go-to prayer when she needed to slow down and resist cussing God out for what hadn't turned out as she had willed. She took deep breaths.

An image of Sadie came into Mary's head. The woman pictured was more serene than the cornered animal she had seemed at the dock. Mary knew she would be happy that Mary had found the necklace and that she could only control telling the truth about what happened. She'd found the necklace and Win had stolen it away again. She couldn't control whether Sadie ever loved her again.

She let herself remember the first time she had placed the necklace around Sadie's warm neck. The memory propelled her out of the apartment, down the stairs, and out the front of the store. With her hands empty but tightly clenched, Mary marched down the sidewalk toward Sadie's apartment.

A caravan of trucks loaded with ride equipment, generators, tents, and carnival workers was parading down Main Street like celebrity floats. The lead truck looked like a renovated luxury camper. Pictured on the side of the truck was a beautiful man in magician garb. Transformation Amusements had arrived.

For once, Mary gave the processional only cursory attention. She didn't scrutinize each face looking for someone who resembled her mother. She didn't wave or speak to anyone. She didn't care if anyone saw her. She didn't feel the obligation to explain herself to anyone other than Sadie. She reasoned that, like the AA material said, she was only responsible for her side of the street.

When she arrived at the door of Sadie's apartment building, she knocked and rang the doorbell for good measure. She stood back on the sidewalk looking up at her window. She was in there. The curtain moved. She had probably checked to see who was at her door making such a racket. If she saw it was Mary at her door, Mary thought, Sadie might not answer the door at all. Or maybe she would. Again, she couldn't control what Sadie thought, felt, or did.

Mary waited. Knocked again. Pressed the off-white button in a rhythmic fashion. Maybe she could annoy the woman into opening the door. She would probably owe Sadie an amends for the incessant ringing and knocking, but she didn't want to yell anything about finding the necklace.

The door opened. Sadie's angry face popped out between the door and doorframe. "What?"

"I found your necklace."

Sadie opened the door wider. Tears came to her eyes. Her anger melted from her face, and she looked at Mary like Mary had invented fire.

"Come in." She took Mary by the hand and pulled her inside the doorway, closed and locked the door. She took Mary into her arms and hugged her tight.

Mary sighed. Despite her racing heart, she felt like her body was being refreshed after a long stretch without food or water. She closed her eyes and put her hands on Sadie—one at the small of her back and one higher between her shoulder blades. Her hands remembered the contour of Sadie's meagerly muscled back. She smelled Sadie's hair. "Hmm. Head and Shoulders."

Sadie leaned back and looked at Mary. "You. I remember you."

"Yep, it's me. You may remember me as a coward."

"I'm sorry I yelled at you."

"There was some truth in what you said."

"Come upstairs."

They walked up the flight of stairs hand in hand as they had all those years ago. Their ascension was slower, the wooden steps were more worn and discolored. They each grabbed a railing with their free hand, but the movement was familiar and calming. Mary wondered, but only for a millisecond, if she would remember how to love Sadie again.

"I can't believe you found it. I mean, I can, that's why I asked you to look for it, but I am still amazed and very relieved." Sadie sat on the couch and patted the cushion next to her.

Mary sat beside Sadie on the couch. "It was dumb luck that I saw it hung up on the dock hardware. Then it was bad luck that caused me to knock it in the water. I'm just glad I found it again. I tried to tell you, but you were in a hurry to get away from me."

"Yeah, that. I'm sorry. I guess I was pretty freaked out. Two men died—one I had pushed in the water and the other someone I knew casually." Sadie turned and pulled her hair away from her neck. "Where is it? Will you put it on me? I thought I'd lost it forever or it was going to condemn me in a murder trial. I wore it at my wedding. I've only ever not worn it a handful of times since you gave it to me."

Mary squirmed even though the couch was cozy and she loved sitting so close to Sadie. She stalled for time but also a clarification. "You wore the necklace when you were married?"

"Of course, I did. I wore it on my wedding day. It's my favorite necklace." Sadie turned back to Mary.

"Didn't Graham object to you wearing jewelry from a former lover?"

"I don't think Graham thought much about my jewelry. He offered that I should pick out my wedding ring and seemed to understand that I didn't want to support the diamond trade." She held out her hand to Mary. "See, it's just a simple gold band much like the one you talked about once upon a time."

Mary held Sadie's left hand in hers. She scanned the ring but focused more intently on her slender fingers and creased, tender skin. "During courtship the great grey shrike—it's a small bird—anyway, the males offer the females food like crickets, lizards, and small animals. Supposedly, more nutritious meals help the female lay more eggs."

Sadie leaned in and kissed Mary's cheek. They looked into each other's eyes and Mary massaged the top of Sadie's hand with her thumb. "Male bowerbirds make complex pavilions of bones, pebbles, and shells. The females inspect the various structures the males have made and choose the most talented architect as their mate."

"You don't say." Sadie kissed Mary's neck.

"Male penguins give the females pebbles to build nests."

"That's all very fascinating." Sadie stopped kissing Mary. "Do you want to continue this zoology lecture? Or do you want to kiss me? I hope you want to kiss me. I believe I proved my case about expedient, explicit romance years ago."

"Yes, you have. And yes, I have wanted to kiss you every day of my life since I met you." Mary cupped her hands lightly around Sadie's face and bowed in to kiss her lips. The kiss was short, a relief. They touched their foreheads together and sighed.

"It's been a long time."

"I've missed you."

"Did you love me?"

"Don't you know? I've always loved you."

"But you must have stopped loving me, right? I mean, you married Graham." Mary pulled back and looked at Sadie.

"I still loved you." Sadie tilted her head as she looked at Mary.

It was like bees were stinging Mary's brain. She was flushed and dizzy. "Did you love Graham?"

Sadie straightened her neck. "Of course, I loved Graham. I married him. We were married for over twenty-five years."

Mary sat back. The air left her body as the back cushion of the couch exhaled along with her.

The silence between them sucked the rest of the air out of the room, first for Mary and then for them both.

"What? Because I loved you, I couldn't have really loved Graham or vice versa? Is this like the conservation of energy law in science? I think love is a different kind of animal or energy."

The wheels in Mary's head were spinning forward and backward and felt about ready to fly off the feeble machine. "He's a man. I'm a woman."

"You say that as if men and women are different species."

"They are." Mary smiled weakly, rolled her eyes. "How could you love us both, really?"

"I guess I'm just lucky." Sadie laughed.

Mary's face flashed more confusion. "This is no joke to me."

"It's no joke to me either. I guess I have the capacity for loving a person no matter what gender they are." Sadie took Mary's hand in both of hers and brought it to her heart. "This is all very hard for you. I see that."

"So, who's to say you won't fall in love with someone else again? Even another man?"

"I guess no one can predict the future, but I have a say in it. I keep my commitments."

"You left me," Mary said. The words were barely audible. She pulled her hand back from Sadie's grasp.

"Mary, your mother left you. I left town, but before I did, I asked you to come with me."

Mary's eyes stung with tears.

Sadie continued. "You were more committed to things here and staying in the same town than trying life with me."

Even as her throat closed and tears streamed down Mary's face, she knew Sadie was telling the truth. But the truth hurt more than the version of reality she had clung to. Sadie had more to say and each statement grieved and bruised Mary.

Sadie sat back and faced forward. She continued in a whisper. "I didn't expect to meet anyone. I wasn't looking for anyone. My heart was still broken, missing you. I always expected you and I would grow old together, maybe even settle back in Whistler in our retirement years. We'd be the old spinster schoolteacher and the grocery lady or whomever you decided to be." Sadie wiped away some of Mary's tears, but it was a Sisyphean effort. The tears kept flowing. "When I met Graham…"

Mary inhaled deeply. Her breath stuttered along to her lungs like when a child has cried so long that their words come out in hiccups. "I missed you too."

"When I met Graham, he made me laugh. It felt so good to laugh again. We were playmates like you and I had been. We were littermates tumbling like puppies. It didn't look like a Viagra commercial with us in side-by-side tubs with the sunset in the background. We took a cooking class and then a bus tour to see an underwhelming performance of *The Music Man*. I thought he might be gay. It was so easy to be around him."

Sadie and Mary laughed. "Gay men do make the best friends."

"Am I right? So true. And it never hurts to have a handsome man on your arm to keep the creepier sorts of men away."

"Yeah, I can see that." Mary couldn't see it for herself. She had never had that kind of relationship with a man. Her father had been her best friend. The men in town had been her customers and colleagues in joint ventures like the Carnival, but she'd never shared more than a project or a conversation with them. The men at her meetings were her fellows. Joey Kay was her lifeline for sobriety. They weren't love interests or playmates.

"Not that all gay men are handsome, just like not all lesbians look like lumberjacks."

Mary looked down at her plaid shirt. *At least it's not flannel.*

"We had so much fun and he was so understanding and kind. I just loved him. It seemed natural as rain to then *love* him. I didn't think I was breaking any sexual orientation rule. The most difficult part was thinking about what you'd think, but I told myself you would want me to be happy." Sadie pressed her hands together. "Was I wrong?"

Mary wasn't certain which thing Sadie was asking about. Was Sadie asking if she was wrong to fall in love with a man or if she was wrong to assume that Mary wanted her to be happy. She didn't answer either query.

"You know, when Graham died I thought the world would just stop. It did stop for me for a while. I was just so sad. I didn't have a reason to get up except to take the dog out. I didn't care about food or housekeeping or working. The thing that changed me, motivated me was that I had a few conversations with dead Graham and then with alive you."

"Huh?" Mary looked up at Sadie.

"I know, it sounds crazy, but I would talk with Graham out loud in my house. It was more of a monologue, of course. I told him how very angry I was that he had died."

Mary spoke through her strangled tears. "It was pretty rotten of him to die."

"He didn't answer me."

"The dead are very disappointing conversationalists at first."

"I know, right? I suppose I didn't let him get a word in edgewise once I started talking, but I had so much to say. I was angry and sad and alone. There was so much to do and it was clumsy and lonely to be doing it all on my own. It reminded me of the old movies where bumbling fools try to move a ladder and crash into every structure and misjudge every small space until the walls and ceilings are cracked and the windows broken. I damaged all the walls and ceilings around me until I saw myself standing alone in the rubble. I talked myself out to Graham. I'm certain he wasn't without sympathy, but he couldn't help me."

"Was that when you began talking to me from a distance?"

"Yes, I'd ask myself, what would Mary say about this or the other."

"Why didn't you just call me?"

"Why didn't you call me? The line runs both directions. My number wasn't unlisted. I didn't change my name. You could have found it if you'd wanted." Sadie sighed. "Sorry. I didn't really expect you would call me. It would have been long distance and you would have judged it an unnecessary expense." She recognized her own sarcasm. "Oops, sorry again." She closed her eyes and when she reopened them, she said, "I didn't call you because I was afraid you wouldn't want to talk to me and that would have killed me."

"So, you talked to me like I was with you?" Mary wiped her eyes and nose on the inside of her shirt.

"Yes. I don't mean to sound like a bumper sticker or a keychain."

"That's okay. I'm in AA. We love bumper stickers and keychain slogans."

"I asked myself what I thought you'd do; and I got the sense you would tell me what I needed to do; and you did. You didn't literally, but the you in my mind told me. Not out loud."

"I get it. What did I say?"

"You told me I could survive."

"Oh, that's all? Didn't I have anything more substantive than that?" Mary slouched and looked down at her lap.

"I know. It sounds simple, but just then it was a profound expression of hope. You told me I could live through losing Graham. My life wasn't over. I had reason to get up beyond toileting the dog. I went back to work. I went back to school for my administrator's license and here I am. I'm not curled up in a whimpering ball, I'm a school superintendent in Whistler, Minnesota, and if you hadn't found that necklace, I may have been a suspect in a murder."

"It sounds a little like my story of getting sober."

"What do you mean? Tell me."

Mary continued looking down at her lap. The only person who knew this story, the uncensored version of this story, was Mary's AA sponsor, Joey Kay.

"Mary, I hope you know that there isn't anything you could tell me that would change my affection for you. I can be mad at you and still love you."

Could that be true? Mary wanted it to be true and she wanted that affection to include being in love. She couldn't control that. She could be honest and pray for help letting go of the outcome. She took Sadie's hand.

"My drinking got even worse after you left. I don't mean it was your fault. It was already pretty bad and worse than you ever knew about. We drunks are sneaky. My sadness and resentment were just another justification to do what I wanted to do anyway, which was to drink. Even Dad was worried. Now that should tell you something right there. He drank a lot, but my drinking left him terrified. He told me as much. I didn't care. I told myself wasn't that the pot calling the kettle black? He was a bigger drunk than me. Besides, in my mind he was to blame for me taking up drinking in the first place. He taught me and modeled persistence of the art every day. I also blamed him for my staying in Whistler. I had to stay with him and run the store. I was the grocery lady martyr, I guess, an unlikely combination and hard to costume.

"He'd had some spells already, small strokes. We didn't know that at the time. The pieces fell together much later. The day he died he had a bigger stroke, but he might have survived if someone had helped him, got him to the hospital faster. He might have lived if I hadn't already been three sheets to the wind and in my room in bed. I'd closed the store early. See, I wasn't always afraid to lose a few dimes.

"I heard him call. I just thought...I don't know what I thought. I stayed in my bed. I fell asleep or passed out. When I woke up and finally dragged myself out of my room, probably to pee or throw up, I found him on the floor. As drunk as I was, I tried to resuscitate him. That's the sensory image I can't get out of my head—the feel of his skin cold and the silence where there should have been breath and jabbering. His eyes, so dead. There's no mistaking dead from alive in your eyes.

"I called 911. It was useless, but I kept pounding on his chest even as the first responders came and saw he was dead, already cold. I cussed those people out for being too slow to get there and for not trying hard enough. You know those first responders are trained volunteers in small towns. I have to face them on the street and in the store knowing I was a complete asshole to them. By all rights they should have turned the paddles on me and shocked me back into my right mind.

"After they took Dad's body Joey Kay was there like he appeared out of thin air. He stayed with me. He asked me if I was finally ready to admit that my life was chaos as long as I continued drinking. I heard his quiet questions between bouts of crying and vomiting. I wanted to be insulted that he could insinuate such a thing, but the evidence was pretty overwhelming.

"I was still drunk, and my dad was dead. I couldn't go to a hospital or detox to dry out because I had a funeral to plan. Joey and his wife, Carolyn, stayed with me, giving me just enough to drink to keep away the awful withdrawal and they got me through Dad's funeral. Then I went into the hospital. Joey knew Dr. Jonas and got me a bed to safely complete my withdrawal. You probably know alcohol withdrawal can kill you. Joey brought me some AA literature, visited me every day, and I haven't had a drink since.

"Little by little I got my life back, but Dad was dead. There was no going back in hopes of saving him. I just live a day at a time and try to be of use to my neighbors. For me, that's running that grocery store, volunteering at the Carnival, and maybe a roof garden. Although the roof garden has lost its luster in recent days." Sadie squeezed Mary's hand and put her head against Mary's shoulder.

"You asked at the lake why you weren't enough for me to get sober. My drinking was never about you not being enough. I'd say that I am sorry I didn't get sober sooner and that would be true, but I also know that it happened as it should have in God's time. My regretting God's timing is just the sort of sneaky idea that might convince me I should drink because woe is me that I didn't stop sooner. I can't risk that first drink. I'm not like the people who can take it or leave it. If I take it, I can't leave it."

Mary wiped her tears on her sleeve. Sadie hadn't kicked her out of the apartment or run away. She hadn't yelled or impotently sworn. "It feels good to sit here with you even if we talk about hard stuff."

"I like it too, Mary." Sadie took her hand. "You said you found the necklace, but you still haven't given it back to me. Is there something wrong? Is it too painful to let me have the necklace again?"

Yes, it was painful, but that wasn't the reason Mary didn't give the necklace to Sadie. How could she tell Sadie that she'd found the necklace and lost it again, thanks to the whims of her bird? Would there have been more kissing? Mary wondered that herself, but she couldn't know because just then Sadie's cell phone rang. It was Judge Tall.

Sadie took the call and then rushed to the door. "Come on. Judge Tall said something awful has happened with her sister. She needs us at her place as quickly as possible."

What about the kissing?

CHAPTER SEVENTEEN

Eden and Purgatory

Mary had never been to the judge's house before in her life and now she had been invited twice in one week. She liked the idea of seeing the lake and property again but would have rather stayed on the couch with Sadie. Add to that, Mary was not used to being summoned anywhere. She didn't join clubs or obligate herself to meetings other than her AA meeting. Were the three of them becoming some sort of club or cult? Again, she found the numbers inflated.

She had never been a joiner. She had never joined the Women's Club even though she respected their work, volunteered at their booth during the Carnival, and cut them breaks by selling the ingredients needed for their various culinary fundraisers at cost. She hadn't been ready to lose money on the deal, and she hadn't signed up for any service club because she feared that her membership would panic other women. She assumed they'd assume she was looking for someone to date.

Did men worry about such a thing? Probably the gay ones did, not that any gay man in Whistler had tipped his hand.

Straight people probably didn't worry about misunderstood intentions, not until the past year at least when so many leaders and celebrities were confronted for their acts of sexual harassment and assumed sexual privilege.

She couldn't stand the embarrassment of conversations that began, "Are you married?" She eschewed attempts at close friendships because she didn't want gossip or people assuming that she was trying to seduce someone. She realized on some level that her fear was like the egocentricity of adolescence and that there was a fair possibility that not everyone in Whistler was focused on her and her sexual preference. To be safe, she kept to herself, ran her store, and survived on the sparse nourishment of acquaintances and a weekly twelve-step meeting and the hope that eventually Sadie Barnes would come back again.

Mary prayed away her resentment that Judge Tall had called and interrupted an intimate time between Sadie and her. After all, hadn't she just prayed for God's will to be done? God bless the old jurist and God's sense of humor. Mary smiled to herself.

Also, she felt she had made headway in her relationship with Sadie and she wasn't about to jeopardize that by refusing to go with her to this emergency. It was a bonus that she could delay admitting having found the necklace and lost it again.

When they arrived, they found Judge Tall in the dining room of her home striding back and forth. The china cups and saucers rattled on the shelves of the hutch. The glass shook in the windows. Judge Tall waved them to join her in the kitchen.

A woman, older than Judge Tall, sat at the small kitchen table dipping her cookie into a cup of coffee. A pitcher of cream and plates of cookies covered the small table where Mary, Sadie, and Judge Tall had had dinner earlier in the week.

"Clara, you remember Sadie. This is Mary from the grocery store. Tell them what you told me," Judge Tall said.

"Well, of course I know Sadie." She stood and offered her warm, wrinkled hand to Mary. "You must be that lesbian storekeeper."

Mary blushed and swallowed hard. "I must be." Her orientation had never been announced so casually and out loud.

She wondered if this was the feeling people of color had when their race was added to every detail about them—the black lawyer, the Hispanic judge, the Asian doctor. She wasn't sure if she should stand and affirm that yes, she was the lesbian shop-owner and who could henceforth be referred to as the lesbo or perhaps Mary could wear a T-shirt with the words, "I'm lesbian" in vinyl letters. She felt she was more than any one label, but this wasn't her party. She stayed quiet and gently shook Clara's hand before she joined her seated at the table.

"I suppose you heard that there's a witness who saw Sadie Barnes down at the dock at the time of the murder," Clara said.

Spittle flew from the judge's mouth. "You ninny, you are the witness!"

"That's right. I'm sorry, dear," she said, turning toward Sadie. "You didn't shoot anyone, did you?"

"No, Clara, but the sheriff might think I did." Sadie smiled at Clara.

"Well, that's nonsense. Somebody has got to talk some reason into that addlebrained sheriff. Amanda?"

"I can't tell the sheriff who to investigate or question," Amanda said.

"But Amanda, what if he charges her with the shooting." Clara lost all color in her face. "I couldn't live…" Judge Tall shoved a plate of cookies into Clara's hands. Immediately Clara was distracted by Rice Krispies Treats, snickerdoodles, and date bars. "Why, aren't these lovely." She smiled broadly at Sadie before tucking into a large date bar.

"Actually, the sheriff called me this morning," Judge Tall said. "He's not charging Sadie, not yet. He wants her to come to the Sheriff's Office and answer some questions voluntarily or…"

"Or what?" Mary asked.

"Or he will ask me to sign a warrant for her arrest." Judge Tall lowered her head.

"That's ridiculous. All they have is that she was seen at the dock that day." Mary kept herself from adding that Sadie was seen by a batty old woman. She put her hand on Sadie's shoulder.

"I didn't kill anyone," Sadie said.

"The sheriff is asking for a warrant to search your apartment, car, and office at school. He asked for a warrant for Mary's property too, but I said that was too far reaching. I'm sorry. I had no legal choice."

"What do they think they'll find?" Mary asked.

"Ideally they think they'll locate both the gun and the cashier's checks, I suppose."

Mary sat next to Clara. "Well, the sheriff can search my store, truck, and bank account. He can do a cavity search. He won't find anything interesting or related to Buddy or Kavanaugh."

"Oh, dear," said Clara.

"So, the sheriff thinks I'm hiding a gun and I shot Buddy?" Sadie looked like she might pass out.

"You don't have a gun, do you?" Mary hated herself for asking, but she didn't want any more surprises.

"Well, that's ridiculous. It must have been me who shot him." Clara dumped her purse out on the table.

"What?" the others said in unison.

Judge Tall took over as usual. "Like that helps the situation. That's a barmy thing to say, even by your standards. Clara, have you become unhinged?"

"What do you mean you shot him?" Sadie attempted to put her hand on Clara's hand, but Clara continued to rummage through the items that she used to have in her purse.

"I can't find my lipstick. I know I had it."

"Oh crap." Mary lowered her head to her hands.

"What?" Judge Tall looked at Mary.

Mary couldn't bring herself to say what she was thinking. She watched Clara examine the detritus that fell from her purse: clean tissues, used tissues, a small red leather wallet, a beaded change purse, peppermint Life Savers, a compact—Avon undoubtedly, a folded blue plastic rain bonnet, a manicure kit… This item distracted Clara for a moment. She clipped the edge of her thumbnail and filed the edge. Gum, a Nut Goodie Bar, and Avon hand cream.

"No lipstick here." Clara shook her head and then raised the purse above her head and shook it like more might be hidden there. Dust, hair, bits of fuzz and fabric filtered through the air onto the table, luckily missing the plates of cookies, coffee cups, and cream pitcher. Clara began replacing the items into her purse.

"Do you wear Beyond Color Revenge?" Mary asked Clara, squinting her eyes and trying to close her ears in fear that Clara would say she did.

"How do you know that?" Judge Tall asked Mary.

"Obviously it's the best shade for her skin tones," Mary said as she rolled her eyes. At her own peril she ignored Judge Tall and sighted in Clara again and asked, "Were you down at the lake that night?"

"Yes, dear. You don't look like you wear much makeup. Do you like my shade?" Clara licked her lips, turned her head, and grinned broadly.

"I found your lipstick under the dock," Mary said.

"Oh, that's a relief. I thought I'd lost it for good. Of course, I could just buy another one from Amanda. She sells Avon you know, dear. But then she'd know I'd already lost the last one."

"How on God's green earth did you lose your lipstick in the lake?" Amanda asked Clara. "You told me you were just driving by when you saw Sadie."

"Oh, don't be cross with me, Amanda."

"It was probably my fault," Sadie chimed in. "I waved at Clara when she was driving by that night and I got entangled with Buddy Latiskee."

Amanda looked like she would stroke out. "Don't tell me you got out of the car and went by the lake?"

"Amanda, is this Mother's date bar recipe? They are delicious." Clara wiped her mouth on a napkin.

"Great, you both could be arrested." Judge Tall picked up a date bar, sat at the table by Clara, and ate it.

Clara put her free hand on top of Amanda's hand, "Amanda, I was out driving, Sadie waved at me, and I went down by the lake, but it's okay. I was with Mr. Ruger."

"Oh, for the love of God!" Amanda lowered her head into her hands. When she raised her head bits of dates and the brown sugar and flour crumble clung to her blueish white mist of hair.

"Who is Mr. Ruger?" Mary asked.

"Don't you worry, Amanda. I buried Mr. Ruger in the garden."

"What?" Mary and Sadie were more befuddled.

"When you say, Ruger, are you talking about a gun?" Mary asked Clara. *Please say it wasn't a gun.*

"Of course, I am, dear."

"What were you doing with your gun out in public?" Amanda asked Clara.

"What are you doing with a gun period?" Mary asked.

"Second Amendment." She smiled. "Oh, I only have the one that shoots anything of consequence, dear. Ruger twenty-twos were all the rage after World War II. My husband had one for hunting and target practice. I kept it after he passed." Clara looked over at Amanda. "I think Robert would be very disappointed that I lost it, but what am I to do?"

"What do you mean? What did you do?" Mary asked.

"Well, I must have shot that Latiskee fellow." Her words dropped like an anchor. The conversation stopped.

Clara seemed unfazed by her admission other than to say, "Have you seen *Orange is the New Black*? I hope I can afford some protection on the cell block. Amanda, I will need lots of money for the commissary. A femme like me doesn't stand a chance." She laughed, touched her hair, and searched her purse again.

"Don't be absurd, Clara." Judge Tall looked stricken. "You aren't going to prison."

Mary was stunned. She wanted to return to her general store, lock herself in, and never talk to anyone other than her pets. The world had gone mad.

Sadie addressed Judge Tall. "Clara is my witness that I didn't shoot Buddy. But if she was there with a gun…"

"Clara couldn't have killed anyone," Judge Tall said.

"She just said she did; and I heard that the sheriff is looking for a twenty-two caliber gun," Mary said. "They're dragging the lake."

"They won't find old Ruger in the lake," Clara said. "At least, I don't think so."

"Just where did you put old Ruger?" Mary asked.

"It's in the garden." Clara pointed out the north window but then turned like a weathervane and pointed west and then turned again and indicated the garden on the south side of the house.

"You don't remember where you put it, do you?" Judge Tall asked.

"I'm quite certain I dug a hole and put it in the garden. The soil was sandy. Possibly. I just might need to look at the gardens for a while to remind me where exactly."

"You people go home." Judge Tall began tidying the table.

"We can't just go home. We need to piece this thing together. We need to know what Clara saw." Mary stood her ground, very much aware of how much shorter she was than Judge Tall. "We need to figure out a way to clear Sadie's name… and Clara's of course."

Mary knew she was challenging the judge. It was understandable that she didn't want her dotty sister to talk anymore but Judge Tall wanted the truth too.

"I doubt Clara knows what she saw." Then Judge Tall turned to Clara. "Clara, so you were out for a drive. You were by the lake. What did you see?"

"All right, let me think. I was wearing a red pantsuit with an ivory shell."

Judge Tall sighed. "You wore that outfit to the lake? What were you thinking?"

"For the moment, let's suspend judgment about wardrobe and help Clara retrace her steps," Mary said.

Judge Tall nodded and Clara attended to Mary's questions. "So, Clara, you had your gun with you when you drove to the lake?"

"Yes, that's right. I put it in this same beige handbag."

"Did you see Buddy?"

"Oh yes, I saw him walk out onto the dock where Sadie was standing."

"Are you sure you saw Sadie?"

"Yes, of course. She was wearing slacks like usual and a T-shirt. She was leaving the dock as Buddy was coming onto it."

"Then what happened, Clara?" Mary asked.

"Sadie waved at me." Clara mimed her big smile and coquettish wave back to Sadie. "Buddy came closer to Sadie like he was going to hug her, but then he was in the water."

Mary bristled thinking of Buddy or any man coming at Sadie. She held her anger in check. "What happened next?"

Clara's recollection slowed. "I guess Sadie went home."

Mary looked at Judge Tall and at Sadie before turning back to Clara. "Did you see Sadie leave?"

"Of course, dear." She smiled. "Didn't I? Oh dear. I did a U-turn and came back by the lake. Then Buddy was all wet talking with that other man on the dock."

"You saw Buddy talking with Kavanaugh?" Mary asked.

"I don't know. Who's Kavanaugh?"

"Big guy, wearing a suit. Did you get out of your car?" Mary sighed. "What did you do next?"

Clara looked blankly at Mary. Then she turned to Judge Tall and was nearly in tears. "What did I do next?"

Clara had hit the ceiling of what she could remember.

"What are you going to do?" Mary asked, looking at Judge Tall. "On TV they'd get a hypnotist to help Clara retrieve her memory."

"This isn't TV." Amanda gathered up plates. "And I don't know or believe in any hypnotists. I'm going to clean up this table and then I am going to take a morning walk through the gardens with my shovel."

Sadie lightly brushed Mary's arm and nodded toward Judge Tall.

Yippy.

"It's already hot. I heard the mosquitoes sharpening their teeth as I came up the sidewalk." Mary hoped her weather and insect pronouncement would delay Judge Tall from scouring the gardens in her upset condition. "I know the time is short, but I have to get back to the store and then attend Buddy's funeral. Then I can come back and look for Mr. Ruger."

Great, first I'm searching for jewelry in lake scum and now I've agreed to dig through the gardens of Judge Tall. This is most certainly payback for my misdeeds in this life and perhaps another life.

Judge Tall said nothing at first. She just looked lovingly at Clara and stroked her sister's forearm as she mulled over the offer, likely reluctantly. Mary knew it was not her style to procrastinate on something that needed doing nor was she used to accepting help. She seemed to prefer demanding righteous labor. She looked out the window, maybe evaluating whether she could tolerate waiting for Mary. She looked at Clara, who was again gaping into her purse like the lipstick or gun might be in there somewhere.

"Fine." Judge Tall placed a second plate of cookies closer to Clara and then crossed her arms over her chest.

"Mary, I'll come with you," Sadie said. "Drop me at my place. I have something that might help us find that gun when we come back."

They left the sisters at the table. Sadie got in the truck with Mary. It was lovely to have her beside her in the truck, but it felt like another lifetime ago when she had been in Sadie's arms— even though it had been just that morning.

"What about my necklace? You haven't given it back. I suspect there is a story that goes with that."

"I found it, like I said. I don't know why but…Win whisked it out of my hand, and I don't know where he put it, yet." Mary attended to her driving with occasional glances at Sadie.

Sadie looked down. After a moment she said, "Thank you for finding it."

CHAPTER EIGHTEEN

Skeletons

After Mary dropped Sadie off, she parked her truck a couple businesses away because the street in front of her store was blocked with kiddie rides. She found Sarah at the store about ready to close up shop for the funeral. She had changed into a dress. She looked more like a grown woman than she had in her jeans and T-shirts.

"Jimmy couldn't make it this morning. Something about one of the younger kids having croup."

"That's fine. We'll just close up."

"It's kind of creepy thinking about a murderer being out there. I can't imagine anyone having a reason to kill Buddy." Sarah put a quote on the chalkboard: "The self-righteous scream judgments against others to hide the noise of skeletons dancing in their own closets."—John Mark Green.

"What if he isn't done yet?" she asked.

"Or she."

"You really think it could be a woman, Mary?"

"Women can play a part in anything, even murder and theft. I guess."

"What do you really think?"

"Gandhi supposedly said 'An eye for an eye leaves the whole world blind.'"

"But what do you say, Mary?"

"I believe..."

Suddenly Win squawked, "Gospel truth."

Mary smiled at the bird. "I will deal with you later. Right now, I'm answering a question that Sarah asked me. Some people say..."

Win said, "Bullshit!"

"Wait a minute, I get it now." Sarah looked as if she'd discovered an uncharted island. "You tip off the bird by the way you begin your sentences. When you say something that you believe Win calls it truth and when you say what you have heard from others Win calls it BS."

"Sarah, you are the smartest, most observant employee I have ever had the honor to work beside. You are correct. That's one thing I've taught this ill-mannered bird on our many nights together. I would be most grateful if you would also use your superior intellect to tell me Win's hiding spots for his stolen treasure."

"Jimmy and I are getting closer to finding at least one of his outdoor spots."

"I'm specifically looking for a necklace he stole right out of my hands."

"I'll keep an eye out."

"Thanks. Back to your original question. I don't believe in violence as a solution. That said, people make mistakes."

"Turning the other cheek is a lot easier philosophy to adopt if you've never been smacked." Sarah sat on her stool. "Do you think people who are violent can ever stop?"

"I have to believe that they can or I get feeling so hopeless. If it's about power and control I believe that people can learn other ways to feel powerful and in control. I'm not saying that their victims should remain practice grounds, but I do think there has to be a place for admission of doing wrong, remorse, and changed behavior. The Christian text calls it repentance and redemption. It's not my job to tell anyone they have to forgive anybody else. But I like to hope that if I hurt somebody"—she swallowed hard, thought of Sadie, and continued—"if I hurt someone I need to believe there would be a path for me to return to my community and be forgiven."

"Can I tell you something?" Sarah asked.

"You can tell me anything."

"It was a lie that Mr. Latiskee shot at people who came to his place. He's not a mean man. Buddy told me his dad was just shy and liked to keep to himself. He had nothing against the people of Whistler, but he didn't trust that somebody from the outside wouldn't steal his sketches of his inventions or his prototypes."

"You knew Buddy pretty well?"

Sarah nodded. She looked at Mary like there was more to say and then there wasn't.

Mary stood in the silence, not exactly knowing what to say next. When she glanced at the clock she realized whatever she might need to say or ask would have to wait. She touched Sarah's shoulder. "Here I am yapping when you have a funeral to get to."

"Are you going too?" Sarah asked.

"I was going to, but I think I won't. We'll talk again. One thing, you know those skeletons from your quote for the day? Somebody has the skeleton of shooting Buddy. Someone, maybe the same person, has the skeleton of those cashier checks. Those skeletons are going to keep being noisy until things are put right."

Sarah looked more pale than usual. Mary chalked it up to the prospect of attending a funeral.

They left through the front of the store, locking the door behind them and leaving a sign that the store would be reopened later in the day.

CHAPTER NINETEEN

Hunting for Mr. Ruger

The carnival carousel—at least the beginnings of one—was blooming outside the general store. Mary nodded and smiled at the workers. She did a double take as she perused them. She noted that many of the women from Transformation Amusements maybe hadn't always been female and she had a similar impression about the men she saw. She envied their strength and fitness and doubted she could have survived such a physically demanding job and emotionally draining circumstances.

Electrical cords snaked across asphalt and connected to huge generators. Little by little the midway was being built and juiced in preparation for show time Friday afternoon. Each carnival ride began as an eighteen-wheeler tractor trailer rectangle that the crew unfurled like they were schooled in metal origami. Other kiddie rides were in various states of construction on the General Store's end of town. Mary smiled when she saw the small boats and miniaturized tractors. She hoped they would skip the pony rides this year. She hated seeing the muscled beasts walk in circles on the hot asphalt with only the storefronts in their lines of vision. She hoped the horses had a rich meditative life, especially if they were working carnivals and fairs.

Mary knew the drill. The rides and carnival booths would spring up along Main Street like spring flowers and then be plucked and put away again after the Carnival. The faster, scarier rides were on the other end of town by the school. The booth where children pulled plastic ducks from a small river of water flowing through aluminum tubs was near her store again. The marking on the bottom of the duck—S, M, and L for small, medium, and large—signified which prize the kid won. There would be a row of gigantic stuffed animals, prominently displayed but dusty from never being won, and crates of cheap toys flanking the back wall of the booth.

As Mary walked away from her store, one of the carnival crew members approached her.

"You own that store?" The woman nodded toward Mary's grocery store.

"Yes, we're closed for a few hours now, but how can I help you?" Mary looked at the woman. She wasn't as young as Mary had first surmised, but she was fit and beautiful in the way movie stars were beautiful and elegant in the earlier days of Hollywood. She wasn't a stick person, but a woman with curves and experience that creased the skin by her eyes and at her neck.

"Andrew, he owns this outfit. He'd like to see you," she said.

"Well, I can be seen at my store almost every day. Right now, I have an errand of mercy, but I will be back later this afternoon with any luck."

"Come to the big trailer when you have a few moments to spare. Andrew would rather meet there." She was a woman of few words, but she smiled kindly. "Nice to meet you." She said it in a way that seemed sincere and not a polite reflex. She turned and went back to the carousel.

Mary got in her truck feeling a bit befuddled on why Andrew, whoever Andrew was, would want to see her. *Probably wants a discount on food for the carnival crew.* She considered the idea briefly and dismissed it even more quickly. She backed her truck down the street and parked in front of the building where Sadie was living. This part of Main Street was open for now. She honked her horn to signal Sadie that her chariot had arrived.

The practice of blaring a horn and waiting in the car for someone seemed rude to Mary, but she did it anyway. She tapped her fingers on the steering wheel more from nerves than impatience. She kept thinking back to the kissing and the stopping of the kissing. There didn't seem any good reason to stop the kissing in Mary's mind.

Add to that her frustration that Win had stolen Sadie's necklace and there were witnesses who placed Sadie at the scene of the murder and Sadie's connection to McConnell Kavanaugh. What was Sarah hiding? What would Mary do if she found Clara's gun? Would Sadie or Judge Tall discourage Mary from telling? Should Mary call the sheriff straightaway?

Sadie exited her building dressed in jeans, a long-sleeved summer blouse, and rubber boots. She held canvas gloves and long-handled contraption.

"Is that what I think it is?"

"I don't know. What do you think it is?"

"A metal detector." Mary's face broke into a huge grin. "Dad had one of those. He loved it. Hardly found anything worth keeping, but the anticipation of maybe finding something valuable propelled him to brandish the thing like he was vacuuming the countryside."

"I thought you'd be impressed. I found this online about a year ago, thought of you, but haven't put it to use yet. I think our gun hunt might be just the right occasion." Sadie placed the metal detector in the truck bed and climbed in the front with Mary. "If we could fly, we could use it to search the trees for where Win took my necklace."

"Yeah, I'm sorry about that, Sadie. I had it in my hand. I heard him say, 'mine,' but he's never taken something out of my hand that I didn't offer to him. Something's gotten into him."

"Maybe Win saw what happened at the lake and is now traumatized."

"Maybe, but why did he take your necklace?" Mary checked her mirrors and pulled away from the curb.

"Maybe he was protecting me."

"Did I tell you he had Kavanaugh's wallet and dropped it on the sheriff's head?"

"You're right. Win could be a snitch."

"I should probably warn him that snitches get stitches. Seriously, I've been going over what we're doing today in my mind since we left Judge Tall's place and I don't know that I'm any clearer."

"What's unclear? We need to find Clara's gun. That will prove that she didn't shoot Buddy." Sadie unbuckled her seat belt and pulled it out again and buckled it.

"What if it proves that Clara did shoot Buddy? Why are you so certain that she didn't do it?"

"Do you honestly believe Clara could have shot someone, let alone shot them off the dock from the street?"

"Maybe she took target practice with her husband, Robert. Have you thought about that?" Mary looked for affirmation from Sadie but got none. "We know she went there because she said she did, and remember, I found her lipstick by the dock where I found your necklace. So she was closer to the dock than just the road." Mary looked both ways before she turned onto Pillsbury Road. "Say we find this gun and it's the right caliber and it's been fired, don't we have a legal and moral obligation to tell what we know to the sheriff?"

Sadie kept silent. Her face turned away from Mary.

Mary thought she knew what Sadie was thinking. She was wondering if Mary felt the same legal and moral obligation to tell the sheriff about Sadie's necklace and her tussle with Buddy at the lake that night. Well, Win had that physical evidence. She watched the groves of trees and swaths of fields pass by her window. "I'm not a snitch, Sadie. Let's just see what we find. I trust that there's a way that justice can be done."

"I just don't believe that justice could ever include sending a kind, old woman like Clara to prison."

"I hope you're right." Before Mary signaled her turn into Judge Tall's drive she said, "Oh, another thing. I think maybe Sarah Hanley is sleeping at my store and I think I know who fathered her baby."

"Why's she sleeping at your store?"

"I don't know for certain, but if I had to guess I'd say that her mom booted her out early. She told me her mom would watch the baby until Sarah finished high school and then Sarah needed to be out on her own—that was how things were done."

"God, how can anything change if children are having babies and their own folks are kicking them out to the street? Some of those same folks don't want contraception taught in the school or available through Planned Parenthood."

As expected, Mary found Judge Tall and her sister already digging in the gardens when she and Sadie arrived. The sisters were in cotton print house dresses. Clara's white slip peeked out below the hem of her dress and swayed a few inches above her navy-blue wellie boots. Both women wore garden hats with mosquito netting covering their faces and necks.

"Any luck?" Mary called to them and waved. She offered each woman a new pair of gardening gloves. Both Clara and Amanda accepted even though they were already wearing gloves.

"Depends on your definition of luck." Amanda removed her hat and wiped her brow with a white kerchief. "No gun, but I have found some volunteer sunflowers and a missing spade." She turned to Clara. "Think, sister. Where exactly did you bury that gun?"

Clara craned her head this way and that way like a satellite dish. She turned in a complete circle and then pointed to another garden. "I think it's resting with the hostas." She marched in the direction she had pointed.

All four women poked, dug, and detected in the hosta garden for the next thirty minutes, recovering nothing but some rusted roofing nails from a building that probably hadn't been upright on the place since before Amanda and Clara's father had bought the property at the turn of the century.

Mary was preoccupied with the Carnival starting that evening and wanted to be done with this seemingly pointless Easter egg hunt. What did Andrew want? She needed to have a word with Sarah. In exasperation Mary tried a new tack. "Clara, let's replay that night again."

Clara rested on her garden spade. "Yes, dear. I was wearing my red pantsuit."

Oh crap. Mary dropped her shovel and quickly picked it up again. "If you ever get questioned by the sheriff, he's going to want to know more than just what you were wearing."

She looked at Mary blankly and then blithely said, "Well, I'll just have to tell the sheriff I shot Buddy and to leave Sadie alone." She wandered off to a garden closer to the house. "I think I buried that gun in the peonies."

The peonies were done for the season and Mary was coming close to the same condition. Frustration and impatience spread quickly between Mary, Sadie, and Judge Tall. At the same time, Mary was more and more worried about what Clara's involvement was with the death of Buddy Latiskee and how her involvement and broken memory might bleed the blame over to Sadie, who was now physically connected to Buddy and through previous contacts connected to Kavanaugh.

"Judge Tall, do you mind if just do a quick cursory look in each of your gardens. I really can't imagine Clara going very far or digging much."

"Search the grounds and house if you need to." Judge Tall waved her arm. "Just find that gun before Clara takes credit for killing Latiskee, Kennedy, and the Lindbergh baby."

Mary felt like a warthog or some foraging beast as she scoured the flowers, shrubs, and grasses for Clara's gun. By the time she'd searched the fourth garden she was hot, sweaty...and successful.

"I found it." She hopped over the two-by-eight piece of wood that bordered the garden and bounded over to where Sadie and Judge Tall stood. Clara was using the metal detector over the bird bath.

The four women clustered together, looking at the gun Mary held up between her thumb and forefinger. Initially there were smiles all around.

"Oh, that's my starting pistol. I wondered where I'd lost that." Clara took the weapon from Mary's hand and fired into the air.

The crack of the gunshot made all the women except Clara duck their heads and cover their ears with their hands. Mary recovered quickly. She took the gun from Clara and threw it across the lawn. "I thought you said you only had one gun. Are you completely out of your mind? Why would you fire that?"

"It's only a starter pistol. It doesn't even fire blanks." Clara bent over and began searching through the ornamental grasses closest to her.

"What are you doing now?" Judge Tall walked over to Clara and leaned over to make eye contact with her.

"Looking for my gun. I wouldn't have taken my starter pistol. That's like taking a knife to a gunfight, it's useless."

"It's worse than useless. It's dangerous. You wave that around and you could get shot. Clara, think. Where did you put that gun?" Amanda pleaded.

"I'm trying, dear. I just don't remember. Maybe I threw it in the lake."

"They're dragging the lake." Mary looked at Judge Tall.

"Uffda."

"No, I think I had my gun with me when I left the dock. I'd spilled my purse. I passed by that other man on the ground."

"What did you say?" Mary asked. "What man on the ground?"

"I don't know, dear. I'd never seen him before. He was big and dressed nicely, but he didn't look well." She shook her head from side to side and said, "Tsk, tsk, tsk."

Mary and Sadie looked at one another and said in unison, "Kavanaugh."

"Who's Kavanaugh?" Clara asked.

"He's the guy from Big Bottom Foods who was trying to buy the barbeque sauce recipe from some sneak in Whistler." Mary resisted the temptation to look at Sadie. Instead, she turned to Clara. "Who was on the dock when you saw Kavanaugh on the ground?"

Clara's face was blank. She looked side to side, like something in the yard might tip her off about what she should remember.

"I think we should head back to town," Mary said. She didn't tell them that even if Clara didn't know who she saw on the dock, Mary had a pretty good idea of who it was. "I'm going to call Deputy Hart and see if she will stop by the store and maybe tell me a little bit about the investigation."

"Don't you dare tell anyone what Clara said. Don't tell about me either for that matter." Sadie looked at Mary. The judge nodded her assent.

Maybe they all could have adjoining cells, because it looked to Mary that one or more of them was going to jail. *"My side of the street, my side of the street,"* she reminded herself. After she dropped Sadie off at her apartment, she called the sheriff dispatch.

CHAPTER TWENTY

The Stash

When Mary returned to the store, she came in through the back. She found Bob Barker by the small bedroom and bath area next to the grocery stock. "What's wrong with you?" Mary called after him. He sniffed at an overnight case that sat on the floor next to the single bed. The bedspread was askew. The dress Sarah had been wearing for the funeral was carelessly thrown across some cardboard boxes. Books towered in piles. Stuffed animals and a laptop were on the dresser. Mary smiled. When she got to the front of the store, Sarah and Jimmy were coming through the front door, excited as puppies.

"I'm sorry, Mary, Jimmy came to open, but I talked him into leaving the store closed a while longer. We found Win's stash!" Sarah was pulling her hair back and restraining it with a hair binder.

Mary was distracted.

"Can we use that ladder behind the store?" Jimmy asked.

"Yeah, why don't you hunt up the ladder, Jimmy. I need to talk with Sarah a moment." Jimmy walked through the store to the back.

"Sarah, did you take me up on my offer about keeping some things here at the store?"

"Yes."

"Did you decide to live in the store?"

"I'm sorry. I meant to tell you. To ask you."

"You aren't in trouble with me. I don't mind. I invited you."

"Mom just won't let up. She hasn't for weeks. If she's not yelling at me for getting pregnant, she's grilling me about the father. When I told her to lay off, she got really mad and kicked me out."

That would have been a good time for Mary to ask her own questions about paternity, but she didn't. "I'm sorry, Sarah. I'm sure your mom means well. She probably doesn't know what to do." Mary saw Jimmy through the front store window. He waited outside holding the ladder.

"She only cares about drinking and her part-time job at the factory. Me being pregnant embarrasses her. I embarrass her."

The bell above the door rang, but Mary paid no attention to which customers entered the store. She gave her attention to Sarah.

"I'm sorry that's how it feels." Mary wanted to tell her from her own experience her mom probably cared quite a bit and if anything, that she felt *she* was the embarrassment, but she doubted Sarah had the room around her big pain to believe such a statement. "You can stay here as long as you need, but I want you to make certain your mom knows where you are. I don't want to cause her worry."

"Okay. Can I go with Jimmy now? We found Win's stash."

"What stash are you talking about?" Deputy Hart stepped out from the frozen food aisle.

Sarah looked at Mary.

"It's okay, Deputy. It's not drugs unless my crow has adopted a new bad habit." Mary turned to Sarah. "Go find what he's stolen. Bring it all back here. I'll explain what's going on to Deputy Hart." Sarah left the store.

Mary had met Deputy Hart before but couldn't exactly say they were friends or even acquaintances. Still, she thought she had a better chance asking her about the case than soliciting Sheriff Spelt.

"Let me explain. As you may know, I have a pet crow named Win. Maybe Sheriff Spelt told you Win found the Big Bottom Foods' man's wallet and nearly dropped it on his head. I don't know how he got it, but I'm curious about what else the kleptomaniac may have hidden. I don't think the bird is strong enough to carry a gun, besides he's a pacifist, but I've asked Sarah and Jimmy to spy on Win and find his hiding places. Apparently, they found another of his caches."

"Is that why you called me?" Deputy Hart asked.

"No. I didn't know they'd had success until I got here just now. I called you because I was hoping you could shed some light on how this investigation is going. You know there's a lot of people depending on this carnival being a success. The missing money has made people reluctant to pick up shifts. I heard that the various booths are being run with skeleton crews and that both the Lions Club and Women's Club are making calls begging people to work and attend."

"Why didn't you call Sheriff Spelt and ask him about the investigation?" Deputy Hart crossed her arms over her chest.

Her question was like a flick in the forehead to Mary. She questioned herself. Why had she thought Deputy Hart was the best bet for information? "Well, that's a fair question. I just thought..." Mary hesitated.

"You thought that since I was a woman I would talk about the investigation or maybe you thought that since I was a woman in law enforcement that we possibly had *other* things in common."

Mary blushed and swallowed hard. "Wow, I don't know that I had all that in my head. You could be right. I read somewhere that there are things a person knows they know and things they know they don't know; and there are things we don't know we know and don't know we don't know. Maybe this is one of those."

"Which?"

"I know I don't know. At any rate, I just thought maybe you'd be less interested in lording authority over me. You could be right that I made some other assumptions too. For that, I am sorry, but I'm not sorry that I'm asking you this question instead of your cranky, idiot boss."

Deputy Hart stood more at ease, looking at Mary. "I'm sorry. It just happens a lot that people assume things about me because I'm a woman and add to that I'm a woman in law enforcement. I'm sorry for jumping on you about it."

"That's fine, you can jump on me. I mean, I'm not asking you to jump on me. Would you like a complimentary soft drink? The cooler behind you is well stocked. Oh, that's not a bribe."

"I will take a bottle of water. Thanks." She grabbed a bottle of water from the drink cooler and took a big gulp. "Do you have some specific question? I can't tell you anything that hasn't already been released to the public."

"I heard that the man from Big Bottom Foods, Kavanaugh, died of a heart attack."

"Appears so. The body didn't show any signs of trauma or foul play."

"Did someone say they saw someone else by the lake?"

"I can tell you that anyone who was at the lake that day is a person of interest. Let me ask you a question."

"Okay, shoot. I don't mean shoot me, just say what you want to say." Mary sat on the stool where Sarah usually sat.

"Chill, Mary. What's your theory of what happened? You seem awfully interested in the details and even expect your pet bird has clues."

"I think I know more about who was around there and didn't kill him than I know about who was there and did."

"If you have information about possible suspects or witnesses you need to come forward with that."

"That's the problem really. They might be suspects or witnesses, but who's to say the sheriff will figure out which is which? No offense to skilled law enforcement, but I'm worried I might say something that leads him to the wrong conclusion."

"It's up to the sheriff and county attorney to determine who to charge. You don't control the process, Mary."

"But if the sheriff and county attorney point their finger at someone that person is going to be guilty in the eyes of most of this community. It will be like a scarlet letter on their chest or an albatross around their neck. There's no turning back from that."

"With all the facts I have confidence that our department will do its best to reach a reasonable conclusion and then the judicial system will do its job of testing that conclusion and determining whether it holds or there is reasonable doubt. Again, you don't control the process." She walked to the blackboard, picked up some chalk and filled in African countries on the map as fast as she could write: Somalia, Ethiopia, Eritrea, Mozambique, Madagascar, South Africa, Zambia, Botswana, Zimbabwe, Rwanda, and Uganda.

How many times had Mary had to make peace with things out of her control that she felt inclined to control just that day? It was a theme in her life and maybe in most people's lives.

"Deputy Hart, you have more faith in the process than I do. Maybe I've watched too much TV. Say, you really know your geography of Africa."

"I'll make a deal with you. You don't have to give me the free candy bar you owe me for filling in this map. Instead, you tell me a hypothetical story. I won't write it as an official report today, but there's nothing that says it can't be some information noodling around in my head as we continue to investigate."

Mary stared at the deputy. Her heart raced and her head hurt. It was all too much. She didn't know if she could trust the deputy, but something needed to break so that this murder could be solved. This news would spread as quickly as other gossip. Then, maybe, everything would move ahead. The Carnival would be a financial success like in years past and maybe Sadie would get back together with her.

"Let's just say hypothetically that a person was at the dock when Buddy came there and Buddy seemed to think that person might be who he was expecting to meet there."

"Go on."

"This person didn't kill Buddy, she or he felt afraid and tried to get past Buddy and in doing so lost a piece of jewelry." *Well, crap. The jewelry loss points to a woman. So much for hypotheticals.*

"Interesting. I'd say that mystery person should come forward and tell their side of the story. If that jewelry was one of the things we found when we dragged the lake it won't look so good for them if the sheriff's department traces that jewelry back to them. Makes them look guilty of withholding evidence or possibly murder."

Mary knew with almost certainty that the necklace would not be found in the lake. Win had taken it. Of course, Win could have dropped it in the lake, but Mary doubted the bird would be that careless. He protected his booty. Still, she began to panic. She didn't want to make things worse for Sadie by having talked to the deputy.

"I'll pass your advice along." Cleaning her side of the street could hurt other people. She wasn't supposed to do that. She decided that maybe she needed to live with the litter on her side of the street a while longer.

"Make certain you do. I don't want to see anyone wrongly accused. The more pieces of the puzzle we have the more likely we will get it right. Tell your friend to help us."

"Did they find the gun?"

"Any gun located in that search would have to be fingerprinted and tested to determine if it was the gun that killed Buddy. I'm not at liberty to say if or how many firearms were recovered."

Mary smiled. "I'm guessing there's a fair number of guns in this town that aren't registered, just passed down from family to family or informally sold. Might be difficult to match a gun to an owner."

"We might have to depend on the morality and goodwill of other citizens to identify any guns we locate." As Deputy Hart was leaving the store Sarah and Jimmy rushed in. She held the door for them, closed it again, and stepped back to the counter.

Sarah and Jimmy were both out of breath and both talking at once.

"We found the stash." Jimmy beamed.

Ever the scientist, Sarah added, "Win probably repurposed a hole a woodpecker had made."

"You won't believe all the things he's collected." Jimmy carried a plastic bag. "A necklace was in with the stash."

Crap. Mary and Deputy Hart exchanged looks.

"Where's my ladder?"

He pointed out the front window, perhaps confused about Mary's sudden preoccupation with the ladder as opposed to the necklace she'd been eager to locate.

"Jimmy, why don't you put the ladder back behind the store where you got it."

Deputy Hart stood, unmoving like a redwood. It appeared she had decided to stay for the unveiling. Mary put up one hand to the deputy and with the other she snatched the bag of booty, squeezing the plastic bag tightly closed.

"That's okay, Deputy. I've got this. I'll pass your message to my friend." Mary was around the counter and standing toe-to-toe with the deputy. She kept the hand with the plastic bag behind her back. "Right now, I need to close my store. It's Friday of the Carnival. I need to find a looser pair of jeans so that I can eat mini donuts, cheese curds, barbequed chicken, hamburgers, and if I'm feeling peckish I may have some pie. I'll get this thing with my bird sorted." Mary flipped the sign to Closed as she opened the door for the deputy. "Come again soon." She smiled.

Deputy Hart didn't smile. She held eye contact with Mary for a moment, put on her hat, and left.

Mary was about jumping out of her skin in anticipation, but she was also cognizant that she had not thought about what she would tell Sarah and Jimmy about the necklace or other items that were potentially in Win's cache.

CHAPTER TWENTY-ONE

My Side of the Street

Mary had locked the store as soon as the deputy was out the door. Jimmy returned to the front counter from the back of the store after he had returned Mary's ladder. Mary addressed her eager staff. "I appreciate what you have done for me. There's a fifty-dollar bill for each of you under the drawer of the till. Now, I need to you to temporarily forget what you did for me and what you found in that hole in the tree. I need to go through this stuff by myself and figure out what it means, but I don't want anyone else to know the specifics until I have time to think."

"Okay, but what about the necklace? It was in the stash." Sarah opened the cash register and retrieved the rewards for herself and Jimmy.

"I will return that necklace to the person who lost it. She's not a killer and has no important connection with what happened to the two dead bodies at the lake." Mary hoped she hadn't just lied. "I need you to trust me about that."

"Okay. Do you think Win knows who killed Buddy?" Sarah asked.

"I think he does."

"Does he know who has the five-thousand-dollar check?"

"I don't know that Win knows that, but I know."

"Who?" Jimmy asked as he pocketed his fifty dollars.

Sarah stared at Mary, her eyes wide like prey.

"That's not for me to tell. I'm only responsible for my side of the street. That person is only responsible for their side of the street. Thanks, kids. I'll probably see you two at the Carnival later."

Jimmy and Sarah left the store together out the front. Sarah locked the door again with her key.

Mary took the plastic bag of detritus to the back of the store, added the booty she'd left in the potato bin, and went upstairs to her apartment. Her dad had been dead for years, but the silence of him not being there still jolted her. It was more than just his physical absence from the space; it was a knowledge that he wasn't physically anywhere for Mary to find him. The smell of his aftershave had faded away long ago. Even the unpleasant rank odor of drink, being drunk and hungover had been diminished by time and disinfectant. Occasionally Mary would smell her own cooking and for a moment believe he was there too, but the silence and eating alone dispelled this illusion in short order.

Her oak ladder-back chair creaked beneath her as Mary sat at the table. Bob Barker plopped onto his dog bed. She dumped the plastic bag out onto the oilcloth-covered, round oak dining table. She spread the items out, sorting them into relative categories: pop tops, twist ties, jewelry, fishing tackle, and paper. She put the fake poppy in the jewelry pile. A crow's reputation for being attracted to shiny things and collecting whatever was more anecdotal than verified science, but Mary's experience with Win supported the folklore just the same.

Sadie's necklace lay before Mary. The chain was still snagged with some wispy, green filament—lake muck—like it had been when Mary found it earlier, but otherwise the necklace looked unharmed. She snatched it up and put it in her pocket. She wanted to go to Sadie's apartment immediately and give it to her. To redeem herself for the earlier fiasco with Win. She wanted to prove herself in that way.

At the same time, she was curious about Win's other treasures. Did the precocious crow hold the clues that solved the mystery at the lake?

The papers were scraps really. All the pieces were white with typed print, but there wasn't a complete sentence on any of them as far as Mary could see.

She spread them out on the table and shifted them around every fifteen seconds or so. To somebody watching it probably looked like she was playing three-card monte with trash. She scrutinized each combination. And then, it hit her.

"Holy shit! Slap my ass and call me Nancy Drew! Bob, do you know what we have here?" Bob Barker looked up at Mary. Bob didn't know. She just smiled. She gathered up the papers and other bits and put them in a bag. "Stay there, Bob. I'll be back. I have another mystery to solve."

CHAPTER TWENTY-TWO

Mothers and Daughters

Mary stood next to her truck, trying to make order in her head of where she should go first, when she was interrupted by a voice she couldn't place but found strangely evocative.

"Hello, Mary?"

She turned to the voice and took in the person. "Yes, I'm Mary."

"Of course. I think I'd recognize you anywhere."

"I'm afraid you have me at a disadvantage. I don't know who you are." Even as she said it, she knew deep inside that it wasn't true. Her heart or soul or some such organ or entity recognized this man even if she couldn't call him by name.

"Mary, Mary, I love saying your name." He smiled and drew nearer to her.

She wasn't afraid or feeling hurried. She stood waiting for the man's advance without fear or a sense of danger. They were the same height, and she could look directly into his kind, brown eyes.

"Andrew?" Mary said in a prayer-like whisper.

"Yes, I am now, but I haven't always been." He put out his hand to Mary. "Before I was ever fully Andrew…"

"Mom?"

This moment, this highly anticipated moment was in front of Mary. It had occurred at Carnival time like she thought it would. She had waited for her mom to come back for longer than she waited for Sadie. She'd waited for this moment her entire conscious life, and just as they were about to embrace, Sarah came bounding to Mary, crying and clinging to her like she'd been running for her life.

"You've got to hide me. My mom…" Sarah looked behind her as if she thought she was being followed. She grabbed onto Mary and hid behind her.

"What about your mom?" Mary asked. "Andrew, this is Sarah, she works for me and lives at the store."

Mary, trance-like, watched him.

"What's the matter, child?" Andrew asked. He stepped forward where he could look into Sarah's eyes.

"My mom's been drinking."

That's not new.

"She made a big scene at the beer garden asking me, yelling for me to tell her who the father of my child is. I told her it didn't matter. I told her I would care for the baby myself," Sarah cried.

"She got even angrier and said I didn't know how it would ruin my life and don't expect to depend on her or pawn my brat off on her to babysit so I could go screw some other loser."

Andrew took a cloth handkerchief from his pocket and began wiping away Sarah's tears, bringing her into his arms with coos and shhhs you'd expect a mother to use with an infant.

Mary watched marveled, slightly jealous and enormously proud.

"I don't know why I said it right then, except you told me I needed to let her know not to worry, but my timing was off. I said I didn't need to depend on her sorry ass parenting or put up with her asshat boyfriends. I was living with you and working at the store and she could just go fuck herself."

Mary could tell Sarah wasn't proud of her reaction to her mom's cruelty. As usual kids blame themselves for the hurt dressed in hatred that a parent's ineptitude can inspire.

"She said there was no way she was going to let me live with a queer and that she'd get the sheriff to arrest you for child molestation. I never said anything like that. I swear."

"Where is she now?" Mary asked. She had worried about misunderstandings, although this specific scenario hadn't come into her head. She had kept herself separate.

"She's drunk and not moving too fast, but I think she's looking for the sheriff and coming to the store."

"Are your belongings in the store?" Andrew asked, releasing Sarah.

Sarah was calmer and continued to wipe tears and snot away from her face. "Yeah, my stuff is in the back of the store where I've been sleeping but it's mostly still packed in a duffel bag. There are a few boxes and books, but nothing I have to have with me every minute."

"Good." Andrew smiled at Sarah.

"Good what? Sarah's mom is on her way over here. Sarah can't go home when her mom is treating her this way and she can't stay at the store if her mom is going to make ugly accusations."

"You're right, she can't, but she can get her stuff and stay at my trailer where she'll be safe. No one would think to look for her there." Andrew looked at Mary like he was looking for assent but also like he was assuring Mary of the soundness of that decision.

"Thanks and all, but who are you?" Sarah asked Andrew.

Mary spoke up. "Andrew is my mom. You'll be safe with him. I'll come to the trailer as soon as I get some of this sorted. It's going to be okay. Let me give you my keys." Mary held out her keys to Andrew.

Sarah pulled her key to the store out of her jeans pocket. "I have my key."

"Unless you or Eddie changed the locks, this should work." Andrew held up a key attached to a tiny, bronzed baby shoe.

"That shoe is too small, but the key should work," Mary said. "You need to keep in mind that Sarah is seventeen. She's still a minor. You incur some risks hiding her."

He winked. "Oh, I like to live dangerously."

"Go," Mary said. "I'll see you in a little while."

Andrew and Sarah let themselves in the back of the store and locked the door behind them. Mary hoped it wouldn't take them long to gather Sarah's necessities and get out the front of the store. She dallied by her truck, still shaken by what had happened and wondering why she was making herself so easy to find. Then she answered her own inquiry. She was waiting for Karen Hanley's wrath because she could face her accuser and tell the truth. Karen may not believe her, but that wasn't her problem. Mary prayed.

Karen came through the alley to the back of Mary's store dragging a reluctant, increasingly impatient sheriff with her.

"There's the queer. What have you done with my daughter?" She pointed at Mary. "You better not have done anything to my daughter," Mrs. Hanley stammered, slurring her words.

"Mrs. Hanley, we've known each other a long time. I would hope you know me well enough that you know I would never hurt Sarah, and I'd never be inappropriately involved with a child."

"I don't know that. Arrest her, Sheriff." Mrs. Hanley gestured with one hand but needed the other hand and arm laced around the sheriff's arm in order to stand.

"Now listen the both of you. I don't know what's going on here." Sheriff Spelt appeared to be trying to extricate himself from Mrs. Hanley's drunken clinging. "Mary, is Sarah at your store?"

"No, she works there and recently she has stayed in a guest room downstairs from my apartment."

"See, Sheriff. I told you. That dyke has a seventeen-year-old girl living with her." Mrs. Hanley sounded venomous. Mary tried to remind herself that the woman was drunk and afraid.

"Sheriff, I told Sarah she could keep some things at the store and use that guest room if she felt unsafe and unwanted at home, but she has never been in my private quarters nor I in her quarters when she was staying there."

"How do you have the nerve to say I don't want my daughter or that she's unsafe with me? Everybody in this town knows your mother left you, probably cuz you're queer."

"Karen, I believe you do want your daughter and that you don't intentionally hurt her, but you are hurting her." There were so many other barbs and retorts that passed through Mary's mind, but being sober and in the program a while helped her not say most of them. The practical side of her just didn't want to have to make amends for them later.

"Sarah's not at the store right now."

"Liar!" The ferocity of that utterance disrupted Mrs. Hanley's already precarious balance. She landed hard on her ass in the alley. "That's assault. Arrest her."

"I can't tell you where she is at this precise moment. I can predict where she will be in the morning. She's scheduled to open the store. She has been reliable about showing up to work since she started. She's saving for her baby and for college."

When Sheriff Spelt offered his hand to Mrs. Hanley to help her up, she kicked him in the shins. He'd had enough. He must have radioed Deputy Hart earlier because she pulled down the alley in a sheriff's car. In two beats Deputy Hart had Mrs. Hanley on her feet, dusted and cuffed.

"Watch your head, Karen, and so help me if you vomit in my cruiser you will be cleaning this car every day until the smell is out." Deputy Hart deposited Mrs. Hanley in the backseat of the cruiser.

Now what? Will I be taken in for questioning regarding Karen's slurs?

"Mary, you and that crow of yours get in the damnedest situations." Sheriff Spelt sighed, removed his hat, and wiped his brow.

"Thank you, Sheriff," Mary said.

"Don't thank me yet. I still need to talk with Sarah Hanley or my deputy will need to. I don't want that Hanley woman accusing us of ignoring her report."

"When I next see Sarah, I will ask her to contact you or Deputy Hart. I don't know when I will next see her. I can give the message to her friend, Jimmy, who also works at the store."

He nodded that she could.

"Honestly, Sheriff, I gave Sarah a job and a place to stay when it got tough at home. There's nothing dirty going on here."

"Oh hell, I know you're no pedophile. If I had to live with that drunk, I'd look for other accommodations as soon as I could. No offense to you having been a drunk yourself."

"No offense taken." Mary smiled. She had never felt more affection for the sheriff than she did at that moment. She almost hugged him. Instead she offered him a gift of sorts.

"Could I meet you at your office tomorrow morning? There's one more thing I need to check on, but I think I might know what happened at the lake and who was there."

Suggest a time later in the morning, please, so I can attend my AA meeting. I'm hanging by a thread.

He looked at Mary for what felt to Mary an extended period of time, but then he said, "Tomorrow at eight a.m. Better make it ten. I have to babysit the beer garden and a bunch a horny teenagers. I won't get home until late. I'll need my beauty rest."

"You looked mighty beautiful to me today, Sheriff. Thanks for your help and for not thinking the worst of me."

The sheriff placed his hand on Mary's shoulder. She felt kindness and support in his touch. "You're all right, Mary Caine, especially now that you aren't drinking."

Mary nodded in agreement.

CHAPTER TWENTY-THREE

Mini Donuts and Deep-fried Cheese Curds

After a brief stop at a couple of vendors, Mary went to Sadie's apartment. She wasn't certain she was welcome there, but she hoped that the things she carried would sweeten the deal. As she rang the bell, she looked toward the upper front window.

Sadie lifted the window sash and called down to Mary, "If you're here to arrest me, accuse me, or express any level of disappointment with me, go blow it out your ass!"

Wow, she used an actual swear word. This is serious.

"I have cheese curds and mini donuts." Mary held the midway fare up in the air for Sadie to see.

"Why didn't you say so?" Sadie closed the window and bounded down the stairs to let Mary in.

"Now before you eat all my cheese curds and mini donuts, I need your help with something."

"There's always a catch with you." Sadie popped a mini donut in her mouth and closed her eyes as she savored the cinnamon- and sugar-coated pastry. They walked up the stairs together, trading bags every five stairs but eating continuously.

"It's diabolical that both these things are so good. Oh, I should probably tell you I had a few wine coolers. They taste like pop—all bubbly—but I feel a little weird." Sadie waved Mary over to join her on the couch.

Mary surprised herself when she said, "We need to sit at the table." When had she ever discouraged sitting on a couch or bed with Sadie Barnes? Never.

"I'm not here to judge it or scold you, but it's very important that you tell me about your connection with McConnell Kavanaugh."

Sadie slumped in her chair at the table, rolled her eyes, and lowered her head into her bag of mini donuts.

"Don't squish them!"

"You said you wouldn't judge."

"I said I wouldn't judge you about your connection to Kavanaugh and this whole barbeque sauce recipe farce. I didn't say anything about not holding you to some standards for your care of mini donuts."

"Okay, okay. I had a class with McConnell Kavanaugh. He was charming, knew a lot about business, and seemed particularly fascinated when I told him about the Whistler Midsummer Carnival and its world-famous barbeque sauce."

"Were you dating him? Oops, sorry if that sounds judgy. I am merely gathering the facts, ma'am."

"No, I wasn't dating him. Yuck. Double yuck since he was married. We were in a small group exercise together. The focus was franchises and franchising. He was very handsy. I'd never date a guy like that."

Mary held her tongue. "Go on."

"That's all there was to it. I had his email on the class list. I never expected to see him again."

"So what happened?"

"The job in Whistler happened." Sadie mined the last bit of sugar, cinnamon, and oil from the mini donuts bag. "Can you make these?"

"Yeah, but why would I when it's Carnival?"

"We could eat these every day, even in winter when it's not Carnival time. We could eat them on all the other 362 days of the year that are not Carnival." Sadie started in on the few remaining cheese curds.

"Yes, we could and we'd both be big as Buicks and have heart disease."

Sadie didn't say anything. She shrugged.

"What? Do you want to be the size of a Buick?"

"They say nothing drives like a Buick."

"So, you had his email and you got the job in Whistler. How did you come to get in touch with him again?"

"I emailed him with my number and told him about the service clubs who ran the Carnival and knew the most about the recipe."

"So Kavanaugh was interested in the recipe and he knew about its connection to the service clubs?"

"Yes, but he was supposed to call me once he'd talked to his people."

"Then you would talk to your people?" It would have been judgy to remind Sadie that she didn't have people in this regard.

"Right, but Kavanaugh never called me." Sadie licked the inside of the cheese curd bag. "Can you make these?"

"Yes, it's safe to say I can cook almost anything, and I specialize in the least healthy recipes. I promise to cook you anything you want for a year if you can just get through this conversation."

"I'm going to hold you to that, Mary Caine."

I hope so.

"If Kavanaugh didn't call you, how did he end up making a deal with someone in Whistler and how did he get the recipe?"

"I don't know. The next thing I heard was that Buddy was shot and Kavanaugh was dead on the shore. I remembered my necklace was somewhere by the lake and I asked you to help me find it. That's all I know except that I know I didn't have gun. I didn't shoot Buddy. I pushed him in the water, but I'm certain he was alive when I left the lake. And I never saw Kavanaugh that night or any other time here in Whistler. Do you believe me?"

Sadie was a little drunk, but Mary knew that wasn't a chronic condition for her. "Do you swear on an endless stack of mini donuts and cheese curds?"

"I do."

"Then I believe you and I think I know what happened." Mary was feeling pretty satisfied with herself as long as she didn't think about Mrs. Hanley calling her a child molester. She could give up running the grocery store and be a detective or private investigator—Whistler's own sleuth.

"Will you meet me at the Sheriff's Office tomorrow at ten a.m.?" Mary stood up from her chair at the table.

"Aren't you getting more donuts and curds and staying here tonight?"

"Not tonight. I think you should get some rest. Maybe keep a bucket or towel by the bed. Those wine coolers have a way sneaking up on amateurs."

What's wrong with me? First, I declined an invite to be cozy on the couch with Sadie and now I'm turning down an overnight. Who turns down an overnight when you've been waiting for it for thirty years? Has spiritual recovery turned me into a celibate lesbian? Is there such an animal?

She leaned over and kissed Sadie's forehead. "I'll see you tomorrow. Oh, one other thing. Sarah's mom made a scene at the Carnival about Sarah staying in the back of my store. Do you think she could stay with you or have your apartment for a while? I'm guessing I could find you suitable lodging with meals." Mary smiled.

"I'll find my extra set of clean sheets. See you tomorrow."

CHAPTER TWENTY-FOUR

Surrender

Mary went to the beer garden. She felt an itchiness as she made her way through the crowd. She saw many friends and neighbors and other people having a good time without being the way she remembered herself being those final years. She flashed prayers and wished everyone all the things she wished for herself: serenity, love, connection, purpose, and sober rides home.

Her second time through the lines of people waiting for beer or chicken Mary saw who she was looking for. She asked Deputy Hart if she could spare a few moments. If there had been hard feelings that Mary hadn't told Deputy Hart everything when they'd met earlier the deputy didn't show it.

"I appreciate that you gave me some space to figure this out in my own time so that I wasn't telling tales that weren't mine to tell."

The deputy nodded, accepting the sentiment.

"I have an appointment with Sheriff Spelt at your headquarters tomorrow morning at ten. I hope you'll be there too. Before that I hope you can check a couple things. I think if you get the information I'm about to tell you about it will clear up both deaths and the missing recipe. You don't even have to tell me the results. I'll tell you everything I know tomorrow, and I'll bring along some other people to help fill in the missing pieces."

Perhaps Deputy Hart was skeptical or maybe she had already figured out what Mary knew. At any rate, she listened to the small list of requests Mary had for investigation that was beyond Mary's access and expertise. Maybe these were things the deputy had already done. Mary didn't know and didn't push for the information. She hadn't always trusted the process, but she trusted her Higher Power to help her accept the process in its perfection and imperfection.

"Are you doing any more investigating on your own tonight, Mary?" Deputy Hart had her thumbs in her service belt and shifted her weight from foot to foot, doubtless tired from the long day, heavy equipment, and hot vest.

"No. No more investigations of death for me tonight. I have one more stop to make before I go home, and although I think it will be an emotional and tough conversation it's a conversation I have been waiting to have for about fifty-three years."

"Wow, too bad procrastination isn't an Olympic event."

"Right? I'd take the gold, the silver, and the bronze."

"Maybe what you have to do couldn't be rushed."

The deputy didn't know how accurate she was. "Yep, there are things that just have to happen in their own sweet time. No sense trying to push the river. God, I hate it when I sound like a bumper sticker."

"No, worries. I don't get to offer much original material in law enforcement either."

"I hope that after tonight and after this other stuff is put to bed tomorrow I can find a more reasonable pace for my life. I want the best that life has to offer without pride, fear, anger, self-pity, greed, or any other emotions that bring pain. Look at me, I'm almost sixty and all grown up."

"Oh, by the way, I called Sarah Hanley on her cell phone. I got the number from her mom's phone."

"Did you reach her? Is she okay?"

"Yeah, she's fine. She said that you were never inappropriate with her in any way. She will come to the office tomorrow to give a sworn statement."

"Thank you, Deputy Hart."

"Good luck, Mary. See you tomorrow."

CHAPTER TWENTY-FIVE

A Story for Another Time

It wasn't difficult for Mary to locate Andrew's trailer. It was the biggest motorhome in the caravan and his picture was decaled on the side next to the Transformation Amusements logo. When Mary looked more closely she saw the various gender symbols, LGBT and trans flags and other symbols she'd need to ask about because they hadn't made it the consciousness of Whistler, Minnesota, or maybe just not to Mary yet.

She knocked on the door. As she waited for a response, she realized that she wasn't sure what she wanted to say, which was weird. In a sense she had anticipated and yearned for this conversation for years. Hadn't she practiced some cogent speech that captured all her feelings? She took a breath and asked herself what she was feeling.

Andrew opened the door a crack. When he saw it was Mary and not the sheriff or the drunken, verbally abusive woman who Sarah described he opened the door widely for Mary. "Are you okay? Did that woman come after you?"

She entered Andrew's trailer. There was no sign of Sarah except for her sneakers on a rug by the door. "I'm okay. Mrs. Hanley took a swing at me. It was a poor effort. The sheriff took care of it. I assume she is in the drunk tank sleeping it off." She chuckled.

"What's so funny?"

"Before five years ago I might have been in the drunk tank with her. Hell, Dad and I could have shared a room in the drunk tank."

"So Eddie drank pretty heavily?" Andrew locked the door and went deeper into the trailer. Mary followed him.

"Yeah. You mean he didn't when you were together?"

"He did. I just thought that maybe he would have cut down since…"

"Since he had a child to raise alone? I'm sorry. Mine and my father's drunken adventures are a story for another day. Is Sarah okay?"

"She's asleep in one of the guest bedrooms. That young woman is exhausted. I'm guessing the details of how she came to be living in the store are a story for another time as well. If I'm not mistaken, you need to hear a story from me and it better be a good one."

Hell, I'm not the one who needs a damned good speech. Let him explain himself. Mary nodded and grinned just a bit. "It had better be a good one."

Mary scanned Andrew's living room. The conversation area had a large, blondish, leather sectional. The piece appeared well-worn and sat comfortably. Mary waited for Andrew to commit to a spot and then sat a fair distance away near an armrest. The distance wasn't meant to be punitive, but Mary was aware that she kept that distance for her own emotional protection. There was no free or speedy express pass to intimacy even between parent and child. At least Mary didn't know of a shortcut, given their situation.

"Can I get you anything?" Andrew started to rise again.

Mary put up her hand. "God no. I already ate mini donuts and cheese curds. Let's just get to some talking first. Any physical hunger or thirst that I may develop feels far removed compared to my need to know why you left us." Mary could already feel herself tearing up and her throat tightening, but she didn't want him to bring her anything or wipe anything. She wanted him to explain what she knew could never adequately be explained to any child, even if that child was nearly sixty years old.

"I am so sorry, Mary." His face was pained. Tears dribbled down his cheeks.

Mary wiped her tears and snot on her own sleeve and shook her head when Andrew again began rising to give her his handkerchief or the box of tissues on the coffee table.

As much as she may have wanted his comfort and craved a mother's solace, she could not accept it. "You were saying you're sorry." She said this in a voice that was flat and more fitting of a follow-up question about someone's vocation as a podiatrist than the confession of a parent who abandoned her child and marriage and arrives decades later with a smile and some version of gender realignment status.

"Yes. I am sorry I left you when you were only a little girl."

"When did you decide you were sorry?" Mary knew from her AA program that she could make this easier for Andrew. That's what she would do if she were receiving a fifth step and someone had the courage and humility to admit to God and another person the exact nature of their wrongs. Was this her mother's amends? Maybe so, but Mary would not allow that amends to add another layer of pain for her.

Mary's pain was already many layers deep, certainly more than lasagna, maybe as many as the foundation of the earth and possibly as many as an old tree. She had layer upon layer of crust covering her mantle and keeping anyone or anything from getting to her core. She had lived impenetrable before and after Sadie. Her succor for so long was alcohol, but it contained no nutrients. Rather, it dulled the pain of loneliness and loss so that she didn't have to feel the molten rage that was a natural product of the pressure and fear that there was something innately wrong with her that her mother had deserted her. One parent left and one parent stayed. No explanation offered by either.

"I was always sorry." Andrew wiped his face with his handkerchief but continued crying.

"But not sorry enough to come back?" Mary heard herself sound so young. She guessed about age six.

"I came back."

"God damn it, I'm almost sixty. You left when I was six. This late arrival hardly counts as great effort." Her rage didn't surprise her. Obviously, it was in there, but she still felt a bit graceless yelling at her mother.

"He didn't tell you." Andrew closed his eyes as he shook his bowed head.

"What? What didn't Dad tell me?" Mary threw her hands in the air, stood up, and paced the short distance from the living room to the galley kitchen and back again. "Did you know Dad set a place setting at the table every night for you? We looked like whackos. Later, he said it was for you or God, whomever returned first. I put my money on God."

"God is always a good bet compared to me. Mary, Eddie wouldn't let me have visits with you."

"You're a grown adult. You were one already when you birthed me. How could anyone keep you from seeing your child?" Mary sat again in her spot on the couch.

"He let me see you from a distance, but he made it clear that if I tried to contact you, he would take me to court and have me committed as insane and he would tell you…"

Mary raked her fingers through her short gray hair, pulling it hard to have some control of her pain. "Tell me what? That you wanted to be a man? Big fucking deal."

"It was a big fucking deal in the fifties." Andrew grew more animated. "It's a big deal now too in most places. I believed I was a man in a woman's body." He ran his hands through his perfectly white hair. "It was different when you were born. There was no visible accepting culture for transgendered people." Andrew stood up. "Being who you were inside if it was different than your God-given anatomy meant losing everything and everyone at that time. I was dying.

"The young trans men and trans women who work for me now have a freedom and community I could only dream about, but certainly couldn't experience or create in Whistler, Minnesota. There are evolving terms and descriptions for every kind of sexuality or gender identification or non-identification than either of us can conceive.

"Even with this worldly façade of tolerance and understanding, the chic Hollywood scene and the bohemian East Coast, 2018 was the deadliest year ever for transgender people. Those crimes weren't just happening in red states. Every day that I live as who I truly am is a subversive act of defiance that there are still plenty of haters—men and women, religious and nonreligious, who are willing to avenge that defiance."

"Was Dad a hater?" She closed her eyes and tried to pray and listen.

"He was hurt and terror-stricken. Sometimes, it's easier to carry those fruits in a basket of anger. He was terribly angry with me." Andrew sat down again but closer to Mary this time. "I know this all sounds like excuses and they are excuses. There's no way to adequately explain or justify a mother leaving her child. All I can tell you was that Eddie wouldn't let me near you if I was my true self and not being my true self made me want to not be, period. I didn't for a minute worry that he would hurt or neglect you. He adored you. He would have died for you, but he also would have killed for you. He would have killed me, if not eventually physically most assuredly spiritually, if I stayed or contacted you as a man.

"For years as I visited Whistler—always at Carnival time but other times too. I watched you from a distance. I let Eddie know I was in town. I thought he would change his mind. I thought he might ask for my help or counsel. When he didn't, I imagined staging a meeting with you like it was chance. In my fantasy we became friends. That's all it was, a dream. I couldn't risk never seeing you again. The gamble of petitioning a court for my rights as a parent was frightening. What if Eddie convinced a judge that I was sick and dangerous? I was a coward. I know how selfish that sounds."

"So why are you being brave now?"

"Part of my increased courage is this business. I own Transformation Amusements. I wanted you to see it and I wanted to see you. Maybe, I am just a selfish parent who wants you to be proud of me."

Whippy fucking deal.

"Dad died years ago. If what you're saying is true, there was no risk of him committing you after he died. Hell, there was no real risk revealing yourself to me once I was an adult or at college. You could have let me decide whether I wanted to have a relationship with you."

"You're right. I wish I wouldn't have wasted so much time. The more years that passed the less I knew what to tell you. I can't have the time back and I can't get it back for you."

Andrew scooted forward from where he sat. "Now is all I have to offer you. I can't even promise you tomorrow because none of us is guaranteed tomorrow."

Mary had heard herself say the same thing, but she didn't mention that to Andrew.

Andrew leaned in, laced his fingers together, his forearms resting on his thighs. It was like he was beseeching Mary with his whole body and what he understood of his soul. "I understand that you may choose to tell me it's too late for us to have a relationship. That I'm too late to ever claim the privilege of being your parent. I hope you can forgive me, but if you can't and you want me to stay away from you, I will respect your decision and never contact you again.

"I hope you will at least think about having some kind of relationship with me. I don't expect your embrace, but I'd welcome that too. These days since our troop came to town I have enjoyed catching a glimpse of you as you left the store or went off with your friend. Someone overheard that her name is Sadie."

It dumbfounded Mary that Andrew knew Sadie's name.

"I saw you together. You look like you are in love."

Mary stared, stunned at Andrew's observation and awareness.

"I am getting off track. I certainly have no standing to ask questions about your affections." Andrew smiled. "I'd like to know about your love life, but that has to be on your terms. I can sustain myself on the memories I've stored. I've lived on less, but part of me has the audacity to hope we could have more and make something new. Maybe something no other mother who left her child, became a man, and came back to that child ever made before."

Mary let her head fall back against the cool leather of the couch where she sat. She heard her neck bones pop and grind. She was so tired. Tired like a lifetime of fatigue had permeated her body.

"You can sleep here tonight. There's plenty of space."

"No, Andrew, I can't. I need to go home. I need to be unconscious in my own apartment with my dog, my cat, my crow, and my wounds. Tonight I can take no further tearing or salve. I just need to sleep at home. I'll find you tomorrow or I won't. I don't yet know which."

Mary scraped herself off the couch. "Thanks for looking after Sarah. She's a good kid. Will you give her a message from me?"

"Of course."

"Tell her that she can use Sadie Barnes's apartment so that she doesn't have to worry about her mom being upset with her living at the store with me."

"It's hard for me to keep my mouth shut. I keep thinking of arguments I want to make to you."

"That's a family trait."

Mary let herself out of the trailer without further conversation or embraces. She did not hear the door of the trailer close nor did she look back. She walked the empty blocks to the midway. She passed the cheese curds and mini donuts stands. She heard the band playing Del Shannon's "Runaway" in the band shell and smelled the barbequed chicken. Her shifts at the chicken shack would be 6 p.m. to close the next two evenings. She imagined the cold beer and heard the faint sounds of someone calling bingo. The kiddies' rides and games outside her store were packed up for the night and the street was quiet save for entangled couples walking back to their cars or carrying sleeping children who were out far past their bedtime. She stood on the steps of her general store and said out loud to no one in particular, "Huh, my mom came back at the Midsummer Carnival to be with me. His name is Andrew."

CHAPTER TWENTY-SIX

The Truth Shall Set You Free

At her early Saturday morning AA meeting Mary talked with her sponsor, Joey Kay. She told him what she planned to do. He reminded her there was no guarantee that the outcome she hoped for would come to pass, but the plan sounded honest and kind. It probably surprised Judge Tall and her sister Clara when Mary and Sadie pulled into the yard at nine thirty that morning. The two sisters were dressed in nightgowns and robes, face cream, and hairnets. It was an image Mary hoped to bury in a remote file drawer in her brain.

She told the sisters unceremoniously that they should get dressed and scrubbed and that they should join Mary and Sadie in Sadie's car, the only vehicle that could fit that combination of passengers. Additionally, they should prepare themselves for a meeting with the sheriff. Judge Tall grumbled. Clara seemed excited about an outing. She dressed hastily in a pink pantsuit and would have left the house with a green facial mask if Sadie hadn't taken her by the elbow and returned her to the powder room.

Clara chattered away on the fifteen-mile trip, reminding the judge to visit her in prison and keep her commissary account full. Judge Tall fretted and sighed between admonishments to her sister to be quiet. Mary made no efforts to console any of them other than to say, "The truth shall set you free. Today, we shall be free."

Deputy Hart exited her cruiser as Sadie parked by the Sheriff's Office. She had two people in tow, as Mary suspected she would. Neither man was cuffed and both assisted the deputy in carrying several bags of evidence—pertinent clues and irrelevant flotsam, some of which had been found in the dragging of Lake Pepin. Mary carried her small paper sack of Win's swag. They all converged on the steps and went into the Sheriff's Office together.

Sheriff Spelt stood behind his desk a moment before realizing that this operation would require a bigger space and more chairs. He led the conspicuous cast of characters into a larger conference room where everyone could see one another as they sat around a big oval table aspiring to be oak but constructed of fiberboard and a thin veneer. Mary ran her hand over the smooth, but cheap surface.

The sheriff called for a woman to join the assembly. "This here is Cindy. She's a stenographer. She will be typing everything said here today. Does anyone have any problem with that? No? Good. She's doing it even if you do object. After we're done here, I expect you will each review and sign the transcript of these proceedings. Yes? Good." He sat down.

"Sheriff, would you mind if I start?" Mary asked.

"Go ahead. It appears to be your party, Mary." Sheriff Spelt laced his fingers together behind his head as if he were a willing spectator.

"Thank you all for coming. I know you all don't necessarily know why you're here. Consider this gathering a sort of bell choir. No white gloves or melodic tunes, but the parts you play are important if we are to get to a harmonious resolution."

"Oh, quit your jibber jabbering and get to the point." Judge Tall folded her arms over her chest.

"Amanda, why didn't we bring cookies?" Clara asked.

One of the men sitting by Deputy Hart blurted a mid-strength cuss word and began standing up to possibly leave.

Deputy Hart quieted and reseated that particular curmudgeon with just a look.

"Okay, let's start with the questions to be answered. Who killed Buddy? Who was Kavanaugh working with? Where's the gun that fired the bullet that shot Buddy? Where's the certified barbeque sauce recipe? Where's the money Kavanaugh paid in advance and what happened to the next installment? Does that about cover it?" Mary looked around the room at those assembled. Although some looked irritated, there seemed to be a general consensus that Mary had hit the most salient points.

"One other thing, Mary." Sheriff Spelt leaned forward. "Why was Kavanaugh's wallet wet?"

"It was wet because Win, my crow, snatched it out of the water where it had been thrown. Speaking of the bits and bobs." Mary lifted the plastic bag of Win's booty and placed it onto the table. She didn't remove any items from it yet. She watched the expressions of each person in the gallery. She noted the fidgeting that betrayed discomfort or rectal itching. She couldn't yet know which for certain.

"Win collects lots of things. Since the deaths he has shown a particular inclination to pilfer things from the shores of Lake Pepin. I think he has been trying to tell not just me but all of us what happened at the lake. It's my fault really. I have put a lot of information in his head about murder and mayhem by introducing him to the works of Alfred Hitchcock.

"This is performance art and will require some show and tell between Deputy Hart and myself. I wish my crow, Win, could be here because he is the witness who was responsible for gathering the evidence I have in this bag."

Deputy Hart nodded and patted the clear plastic evidence bags in front of her. Several of which contained handguns.

Clara became immediately enthralled with one of the bags and called out like she was claiming a bingo. "There's Mr. Ruger."

Deputy Hart knew exactly what Clara meant and slid that bag across the table for Clara's closer perusal. "Is that your gun, Clara?"

"Yes, it belonged to my husband. I've been keeping it for him."

"Do we need a lawyer?" Judge Tall asked.

"Aren't you a lawyer?" Sheriff Spelt asked.

"Yes, I am, but as the saying goes, 'She who represents herself has a fool for a client."

"Deputy Hart," Mary interceded. "Was that Ruger fired recently?"

"No. It hasn't been fired in years. The firing pin is gone, and the action is rusty."

"Clara, that's your Ruger, but you didn't shoot Buddy with it," Mary assured her. "But hang in there with us. You have some important notes to play."

She continued, "McConnell Kavanaugh got the idea that the Whistler Midsummer Carnival barbeque sauce was available for purchase." People nodded. "Sadie, would you tell everyone how he got that idea?"

Sadie looked at the people around the table. She hoped that admitting what she did wouldn't result in both scorn and unemployment. "I met Kavanaugh in a business class we were both taking at the university. I was the one who told him about the great barbeque sauce recipe."

Gasps and nods came from several people at the table.

"I wish that was all I did." Sadie's face looked like she had been slapped. She had already endured Mary's shaming for her actions and now she must contend with the contorted, frowny, angered expressions of more people from Whistler. With candor and openheartedness, she continued her confession. "Later, I contacted him to see if his company had any interest in buying the recipe."

More gasps and groans emanated from the assembly.

"I meant only if the town was interested in selling it. I wasn't attempting to sell the recipe or take their money myself." She surveyed the glares and stares. "I don't even know the recipe.

Mary told me her dad knew it, but if he told me he'd have to kill me. I never asked. And he's dead now."

Judge Tall pounced, "I can vouch for what she is saying—not all that nonsense about someone needing to kill her but the rest of it. She was only inquiring on the feasibility of the sale of the recipe. There was no intent to sell it behind anyone's back. I will swear to that."

"Sadie, did you ever have contact with Kavanaugh again after that email inquiry?" Mary continued pointing at each bell ringer in turn.

"No, I did not."

"But there's a witness who puts you at the lake the night the two men died. Were you at the lake that night Buddy was killed and Kavanaugh died of a heart attack?" Mary thought to herself that she would have made a pretty fine attorney. She wondered if sixty-year-old people ever ventured to law school. Law school was very expensive.

"Yes, I stopped by the dock to enjoy the lake view and do some thinking."

Mary wanted to ask Sadie if she thought of her that day. She wanted to know if Sadie was contemplating the two of them loving one another again or was she thinking about business. She didn't ask those questions. She asked, "Who did you see at the lake?"

"I was already on the dock looking at the lake when Buddy Latiskee rushed up to me. I saw him first. He asked me if I 'brought it.' He said something vulgar about my butt."

"Did you see anyone else at the lake?"

Before Sadie answered Mary detected more squirming at the table. She didn't call the person out but waited for Sadie's answer.

"Yes, I saw Clara driving by in her car. We waved at one another."

Clara again mimicked the social exchange, looking very proud.

"Then what happened?"

"I'm not proud of this, but I pushed past Buddy and inadvertently or possibly very purposefully shoved him off the dock. The water was shallow. I didn't think I could have done him any harm other than soaking his clothes."

"What did you do next?"

"I left the dock."

"Sadie, was Buddy alive when you left?"

"Yes, he most certainly was." Sadie crossed her arms, indignant.

"Did you leave or lose anything at the lake that is evidence of your presence there?"

"Yes, I lost a gold chain and locket."

"This jewelry was important to you?" Mary knew she was weaving off course, but what was the fun of being the bell choir director without adding a flourish where no other has seen the need?

"Mary, you know very well that necklace was important to me. You gave it to me over thirty years ago when you loved me. Our initials are engraved on it."

There were some agonized expressions in the gallery, but Mary didn't care. She loved hearing Sadie say every one of those words out loud with witnesses. She dug into the bag she had brought with her. "Is this your necklace?" She slid it to Sadie.

"Yes, yes, where did you find it again?" Sadie removed the lake scum-like green web that was caught in the chain. She fiddled with the clasp, put the necklace around her neck, and glowed at Mary.

"I originally found that necklace under the dock in the shallow water at Lake Pepin. I found it exactly where Sadie had said she lost it when she tussled with Buddy. My crow, Win, took the necklace out of my hand before I could turn it in to the Sheriff's Department or return it to Ms. Barnes. Later my employees, Sarah Hanley and Jimmy Royce, found Win's hiding spot and retrieved this necklace and brought it to me."

The sheriff smiled and seemed to be enjoying himself. "Careful, Deputy Hart, you better step up your game or I'll deputize that bird." The humor broke the tension.

Mary turned her attention to the eldest member of the bell choir.

"Clara, what did you see the night Buddy was killed?"

"Well…" Clara sat up straighter in her chair. Mary suspected Judge Tall held her breath and ordered God to keep Clara coherent. "I wore my red pantsuit. That's not important. I saw Sadie. She waved at me. I saw Sadie and that Buddy fellow run into each other and Buddy fell in the lake. I didn't stop right then because there wasn't parking on that side of the street and Amanda told me that I can't just swerve over to the other and park just because it's convenient." Clara looked at her sister. Judge Tall nodded. Her approval and affection shown on the old umpire's face.

"I drove away and did a U-turn and came back and parked lakeside. I had Mr. Ruger with me, in my purse." She looked around the table. "Mr. Ruger is the name I gave my gun. I didn't have a man with me." When it seemed that Clara had accepted the audience's acceptance of her clarification, she continued. "I started to get out of the Chevrolet. I wanted to speak to Sadie. She's such a lovely girl and do you know she has read all the great American novels of the nineteenth century?"

Judge Tall cleared her throat.

"But of course, that's not important. I must tell what happened." She sighed. "Let me think. I parked. I walked toward the dock. I had my purse with me. Sadie was gone. I was surprised, but I guess it's no surprise that it must have taken me a while to park, get out of my car, and walk down there. I'm not the sprite I used to be in my sixties." Clara gathered her thoughts like individual posies. "I was going to turn around and go back to my car, but when I reached the dock, Buddy was there swearing. Bless his heart when he saw me, he apologized for his language. He wrung the water out of his shirttails and struggled out of the shallow water.

"He was so soaked I think I laughed at the way his pants, you know, clung to him in an unflattering way. I dropped my purse and it spilled onto the shoreline." She turned to her sister. "That must have been when I lost my lipstick."

Judge Tall rolled her eyes and said, "Well, good. At least the mystery of your lost lipstick is solved."

"Actually, that is an important tidbit," Mary interjected. "You see, when I found Sadie's necklace by the dock the first time, I also found Clara's lipstick. Go on, Clara, did you see anyone other than Buddy at the lake?"

"Let me think. Buddy helped me pick up my purse. He was very wet, but he seemed like a nice man. After he gave me my purse I began walking back to my car. When I reached the road, I turned back to wave at Buddy. He was awfully nice once he quit swearing. Buddy was out of the water and there was another man talking to Buddy."

"Was the second man talking with Buddy Mr. Kavanaugh?"

"No, dear. The big fellow in the suit was just approaching the picnic area. I didn't know his name then, but I've seen his picture now. I saw him on the lake shore."

"Then what happened?"

"Then that man over there…" Clara pointed to Mayor Carl.

CHAPTER TWENTY-SEVEN

Another Dissatisfied Customer

The room fell silent except that Mary thought she could hear Mayor Carl's bowels clench.

"What was Mayor Carl doing?" Mary asked.

"He threw his arms up and down, stomped on the dock, and yelled at the man on the shore and cursed at Buddy, who was back on the dock again."

"Let's make sure we have the details straight, Clara. Sadie had left, Buddy was alive on the dock being cussed out by Mayor Carl, and Kavanaugh was on the shore? Is that correct?"

"Yes, dear."

Mayor Carl's eyes darted around the room and in his skull like he might have been a slot machine in another life.

"I looked back when I got to my car. Buddy was in the water again and the man on the shore fell over."

Mayor Carl lowered his head.

Mary dug in her bag again and pulled out several pieces of white paper and placed them in front of Mayor Carl.

"cups"

"li sauce"

"oil"

"5 gallon pai"

"/2 black"

"mon ju"

"8-10# su"

"onion flakes"

"Do these scrapes of paper mean anything to you, Mayor?" Mary asked him.

He squirmed and squinted, hemmed and hawed, and finally the truth fell out accidently. "It could be parts of a recipe."

"Good. Any chance these could be parts of Whistler's Carnival barbeque sauce recipe?"

He started to speak several times but gulped air instead. He looked at the papers more closely. "Yes, that's possible. Of course you heard yourself that everyone in town knows that recipe."

"Yep, I remember the Lions Club members bringing up that point." Mary brought out another piece of white paper. "Would you say this paper matches those other papers?"

"Yes, but I don't know what that matters. That last one is blank." He raised his eyebrows as he scanned the papers before him and dismissed the last addition with a wave of his hand.

"Oops, I had it upside down. See this here? That's a raised seal. This copy of the recipe was certified. See that?"

"So it is." Mayor Carl nodded his head as his face flushed, darker and darker, approaching a purple that didn't look comfortable on a fruit let alone a man in his late sixties. "Mary Caine, what are you getting at? I've had just about enough of this poor man's excuse for Sherlock Holmes." He stood to leave.

Deputy Hart said, "Sit down."

He did.

Mary reached again into her bag and placed a faded red paper poppy in front of Mayor Carl. "I hardly recognize you without your lapel poppy. How long has that been missing?"

He reached for it. He nearly picked it up and put it back in the green stained hole in his lapel. He caught himself. He looked at Mary with contempt, but mostly desperation.

"It's time, Mayor Carl." Mary touched his hand as it trembled on the table. "You served your country with honor and you have served this town. It's time you show that same bravery and tell what happened that night."

"It was Buddy's fault. He was weak for temptation. Just ask that girl who works for you." Mayor Carl adjusted himself, marshalling righteous indignation. "Buddy was there in the office the day Kavanaugh called me at the Lions Club. I don't know how he got my number. I guess he got wind of my standing in the community. Kavanaugh asked for a meeting to talk about Big Bottom Foods acquiring the barbeque sauce recipe. I told Kavanaugh he could shove his offer up his ass.

"Buddy, he heard the whole thing. He was working on a bit of remodeling there in the office." Mayor Carl read the room as he talked. "Buddy asked me what it was about and I told him what the man wanted. I told how that wasn't going to happen or if it did it would be over my dead body."

"Did you give Buddy the recipe?" Mary asked.

"I did not. He stole it. Well, you can't exactly call it stealing, but I suppose it amounts to the same thing. Buddy was rebuilding all the cabinets. I showed him the recipe and told him which cabinet to lock it in." Just when Mary thought Mayor Carl's self-righteousness was leaking away, he added, "I never thought he'd take the thing and call Big Bottom Foods himself. Fault me for trusting people." He said it like he had personally been cheated.

"The next thing I know, I'm getting a message on my phone from Kavanaugh that he's running late for our meeting. Our meeting. I didn't schedule no damned meeting with Kavanaugh on the dock at Lake Pepin. No way. I thought, what in the hell? Then he says that he had good news. The trials went well. I didn't know what that was about. Then Kavanaugh said that he'd have the rest of the money for me when he saw me that evening. I checked the cabinet. Sure shit, the recipe was gone. I figured it had to be Buddy, but the only way to know for sure was to go to the meeting."

Deputy Hart took over the interview. "Before you say any more, I need to remind you that anything you say can and will be used against you in a court of law. Do you want to continue, sir, or would you like an attorney?"

He sighed. "I don't need an attorney."

"Why didn't you call law enforcement?" Sheriff Spelt asked.

Mayor Carl scratched his head, but the answer was nowhere to be found in his hair.

"What did you do next, Mayor Carl?" Deputy Hart asked.

"I walked to the lake to see who it was meeting with Kavanaugh. I hid in the trees on the north side of the picnic area. I saw the teacher lady on the dock and then Buddy came. I thought what in the hell? Which one of them is the fink?" He pointed at Clara. "I saw Clara in her car, but I doubted she was in on it."

"Go on." Deputy Hart took notes.

"The teacher and Buddy wrestled some and she pushed him into the water. Then she left in a hurry off the lakeshore. Then before I could get down to Buddy, Clara was there yapping and crawling on the ground picking up the crap she dropped from her purse. By the time she left a big Oldsmobile pulls up and a guy in a suit gets out. I figure that's the Big Bottom guy, right?"

"I hustled to get to Buddy before that guy came with a bunch of money." He lowered his eyes before he spoke again. His next words were said to the sheriff. "I just planned to scare him. I planned to tell Buddy he couldn't do such a thing to the town."

He wiped his face with his hand. He beheld each face around the table. Maybe he was looking for mercy or at least some understanding.

"You brought your gun?" Deputy Hart was methodical.

He nodded. "Hell, you know I was carrying that thing with me everywhere in those days."

"Where is your gun now, sir?"

Mayor Carl glanced at his belt like he expected his .22 to be protruding from his gut like it had before that night.

"I lost my gun."

Deputy Hart pushed another evidence bag in front of Mayor Carl. "Is this your gun?"

"Could be. It looks like it. I'm not sure."

"It has the initials CC carved into the wooden grip. What is your full name, sir?"

He swallowed and set his jaw but answered. "My given name is Carl Carlson."

"What happened on the dock, Mayor Carl? How did you come to shoot Buddy Latiskee?" Sheriff Spelt continued.

"Buddy was on the dock. He had the certified recipe in his hands. He said, 'Lucky I was smart enough to put this valuable document in a Ziplock bag.' He took the recipe out of the bag and waved it at me. I told him he needed to give back the money he took already and stop the deal with Big Bottom Foods. Buddy said, 'Hell no, that money's already spent.' He said he gave it to his girlfriend and the baby they were expecting. He was going to get the rest of that money and help his girlfriend have the education she deserved." Mayor Carl looked around the table at the people staring at him.

"He pulled a gun."

"What?" Mary asked.

"Buddy had a gun?" the sheriff asked.

Scattered conversation erupted in the room.

"Everyone, quiet," Deputy Hart said. "Is it your contention that Buddy Latiskee also had a gun, Mayor?"

"It's not just my contention? It's the truth. He had the recipe in one hand and that gun in the other hand." Mayor Carl pointed to an evidence bag on the table.

"He had Mr. Ruger?" Mary asked.

"Yes, I didn't know it had a name at the time, but it was that gun."

"Go on with your story," Sheriff Spelt said.

"I thought Buddy would respect my authority and standing in the community. He reached out. I thought he was going to give me the recipe, but he had that gun. He had a gun, so I pulled out mine. We were close together on that narrow dock by that time. I went for the recipe and my gun went off. The next thing I know I'm standing on the dock with my gun in one hand and the certified copy of the recipe in my other hand.

Then that maniac vulture of yours swooped down, Mary, and tore the paper out of my hand and flew off into the trees. I threw my gun at the crow, but I pitched that about as well as you pitched in high school, Sheriff. My gun went into the water."

"What about Buddy?" Mary asked.

"He was in the water. He was shot in the neck. I could tell there was nothing to do for him." Mayor Carl's voice cracked like the gravity of his actions was finally catching up with him. "I didn't see where his gun landed."

"I looked back at the parking and picnic area to see how far Kavanaugh had gotten. You know, I was wondering if he saw what happened. He stood a little ways from the shoreline. He looked shocked—a bit a green actually. Next moment he's flat on his back, staring up at the sky. Dead. I checked his pulse. He was gone."

I bet you checked his pockets too.

The people around the table stared at Mayor Carl in disbelief. "I didn't know what to do. I panicked. I took Kavanaugh's wallet and threw that in the lake. I thought that would buy some time and maybe there'd be no obvious connection between me and Big Bottom Foods."

Nobody spoke.

"Okay, quit looking at me like that. I admit it. I searched Kavanaugh for the check he'd brought—see, I was afraid that Buddy had told him he was me and that my name would be on the check and people would think I cheated the town."

"Where's the check now?" Deputy Hart asked.

Mayor Carl reluctantly dug it out of his back pocket. "It's a cashier's check. I didn't know what to do."

"Why didn't you just give it back, dear?" Clara looked at him with doe eyes.

"I couldn't." He turned to Mary. "You heard them at the store. Nobody was going to forgive anyone with that check. I couldn't prove it was Buddy and not me. I didn't know how to give it back or get it into the general fund—either way people'd think I tried to sell the recipe. I never would. Then I got invited to this party. The jig was up."

Through it all, the other man at the table, Bruce Johnson, the president of the Lions Club, had listened and stayed quiet. He had been invited because the service club had the most to lose if the deaths and recipe conundrum was not solved. Disappointment shown on his face as he spoke. "Mayor Carl, I wish you had come to the sheriff, the deputy, or somebody to put this record straight earlier. I don't think there's any repair possible for the volunteers and attendees we lost this year. Our charitable obligations will likely go unmet. Even if we could keep that money, which we can't, I don't think we would even meet what we had hoped to give to the two most excellent seniors."

Mary ached hearing that news and thinking of Sarah and Jimmy.

Johnson continued, "We can give this money back to Big Bottom Foods and hope they don't pursue a case against us, but I'm pretty certain they are going to want the missing five thousand in addition to suing our asses."

"I am so sorry, Bruce. I tried to stop this thing," Mayor Carl said. "I love this town. Instead of stopping anything I sent it off the rails. Buddy is dead."

Mary felt sorry for Mayor Carl. She believed he was well-intended as so many had been, but the results were the same.

Sheriff Spelt stood up. "About that five-thousand-dollar check, it was turned into the Sheriff's Office earlier today with an apology for not doing it sooner. Buddy had given the check to his girlfriend. He wanted to support a family. He wasn't expecting to have a girlfriend expecting so soon. He hadn't told his folks. I think that's what inspired his attempted shortcut to wealth.

"I want to thank all of you for coming forward coerced or otherwise. We need to get formal statements from each of you." He turned specifically to Mayor Carl. "I think I hear you saying that you hadn't gone to the lake with the intention of any bodily harm. It was the struggle between you and Buddy, Buddy also having a gun, that lead to the death of Buddy Latiskee?"

Deputy Hart slowed the rush to acquittal. "Just how did Buddy end up with Clara's gun?"

"I think I know that," Mary said. "Remember Clara saying how she had Mr. Ruger in her purse and that she spilled her purse by the shoreline when she was laughing at Buddy's soaked condition? She said he helped her pick up her items. They missed the lipstick I found when I searched for Sadie's necklace, but that would have been an opportune time for Buddy to see and keep Clara's gun."

There was no way to prove Mary's theory, but both the sheriff and deputy seemed satisfied. The point was that the gun had ended up in the water, but it couldn't have been fired and wasn't.

"Will you have to bring charges against Buddy for attempting to sell the recipe?" Mary asked. "I mean, can you bring charges against a dead man? And it's not like he has an estate."

"The county attorney decides who gets charged and who ain't. I just bring him the evidence." Sheriff Spelt hitched up his pants. "It will have to get out that Buddy did what he did, but as far as I'm concerned Buddy already got more punishment than that young man probably deserved. I'll get that five-thousand-dollar check back to the smartasses at Big Ass Foods and we can close this chapter of the Whistler crime wave. I'm just glad no more had to die. Law enforcement is a burdensome occupation." He patted Deputy Hart on the shoulder.

Deputy Hart glanced at Mary briefly and looked down. Mary hoped that the deputy saw the sheriff's actions like she did—as a moment of grace.

While Sadie gathered Judge Tall and Clara, Mary grabbed a word with Bruce Johnson. "Say, do you think you'd mind making it very clear to any who ask that Sadie wasn't stealing. She honestly thought she was investigating a way to bring money to Whistler, not herself."

"I'll spread the word, but see if you can get her to sign up for working some the shifts next year." Bruce smiled.

"You can count on both of us." Mary handed Bruce a sealed envelope. "Read this when you get back to town, okay?"

CHAPTER TWENTY-EIGHT

Less Money and a New Roommate

After Mary and Sadie had signed their statements and returned Judge Tall and Clara to their home, Sadie drove Mary back to town. Day two of the Carnival was in full swing, but Mary and Sadie lingered in Sadie's car, each mulling over the events of the past couple hours and weeks.

"Judge Tall was very impressed with your crime-solving ability."

Mary scoffed.

"I'm serious. I think there is a huge box of Avon coming your way."

"Could be worse. Could be lutefisk. I'll just mark that for resale and display it between the bug dope and spray for athlete's foot."

Sadie lightly punched Mary's shoulder. "I feel bad about there not being enough money made at the Carnival to cover the charitable obligations especially the scholarships," she said.

"Not to worry," Mary said. "Those scholarships and the other obligations will be met."

"How? What do you mean?"

"I told Bruce Johnson that it just so happens that I know someone who no longer has the added expense of a roof garden project and who happens to have a fortune, thanks to medical cheese."

"No! You're going to use your money for the scholarships?"

"Yeah, this town has given me more than I can ever repay when I was a drunk and double since I've been sober. I think it was Francis of Assisi who said, 'Wear the world like a loose garment.' I'm ready to hold less tightly to much of what I have clenched before—except for you, of course. You, I want to hold tightly." Mary took Sadie's hand and kissed it.

"That can be arranged." Sadie rested her head against Mary's shoulder. "You know, Mary, Mrs. Hanley isn't going to be any more pleased with me taking in Sarah. After all I'm lesbian too, plus I am a person of authority at school."

"What are you saying? I can't tell Sarah she'll have no place to live. She did the right thing and gave the cashier's check Buddy gave to her to the sheriff."

"Well, she can have my apartment. I'll sublet it to her for a dollar a month."

"Well, that's a relief. I visited Mrs. Hanley at detox today. She wouldn't talk with me, but Joey Kay was with her and he told me that she gave her permission for Sarah to live at your apartment while she's in chemical dependency treatment."

"Mrs. Hanley is going to get sober?"

"Looks like. I need to talk to Sarah. I'm hoping she'll take a ride with me out to see Lois and Martin Latiskee. I think knowing they are expecting a new grandchild may go a fair distance in their long road of grief."

"You know, Mary, if Sarah sublets my apartment, I will need a place to live."

"You aren't thinking of moving in with Judge Tall, are you?"

Sadie tried to punch Mary in the shoulder, but Mary caught Sadie's fist and used her momentum to bring Sadie into her arms. She kissed Sadie's neck and buried her face there, necking like teenagers in the front seat of Sadie's car. "Could we just stay like this for a hundred years?"

"That works for me. Well, not really. This steering wheel is in the way. I can't hold you properly in this confined space. Mind if I stay at your place tonight and that next hundred years? I want to know more about your loose garments." Sadie kissed Mary.

"Actually, you're going to have to ask my mom for my hand in marriage and make an honest woman out of me."

"Get out! You're kidding. Your mom? When were you going to tell me that? Your mom came back at Carnival?"

"Yep, his name is Andrew. It's a long story. I'll tell it to you over some cheese curds."

"Mini donuts too?"

"Yep, and the best damn barbequed chicken in the world."

Other Books by Nancy Hedin

Bend
Stray
Rise

About the Author

Nancy J. Hedin is the author of *Bend*, published by Angler Fish, an imprint of Riptide Publishing.

Hedin's poetry and prose have appeared in *Sleet Magazine; Rock, Paper, Scissors, Healing Woman, The Phoenix*, and *The Midway Monitor*. She has an MFA in Creative Writing from Hamline University. She works as a mental health professional in St. Paul. Nancy and her wife and two daughters live in the Twin Cities.

Bella Books, Inc.

Women. Books. Even Better Together.

P.O. Box 10543
Tallahassee, FL 32302

Phone: 800-729-4992
www.bellabooks.com